Having Her Cake and Loving It

Nneka Bilal

iUniverse LLC
Bloomington

HAVING HER CAKE AND LOVING IT

This is a work of fiction. All of the characters, names, incidents, organizations, and dialogue in this novel are either the products of the author's imagination or are used fictitiously.

iUniverse books may be ordered through booksellers or by contacting:

iUniverse
1663 Liberty Drive
Bloomington, IN 47403
www.iuniverse.com
1-800-Authors (1-800-288-4677)

ISBN: 978-1-4917-0923-8 (sc)
ISBN: 978-1-4917-0925-2 (hc)
ISBN: 978-1-4917-0924-5 (e)

Library of Congress Control Number: 2013917356

Printed in the United States of America.

iUniverse rev. date: 10/07/2013

Chapter One

The outlaw curled Ebony's body like she was a pair of dumbbells. Up, down, up, down rubbing her against his well-oiled body. She grabbed his bald head to steady herself. The crowd of horny ladies screamed in excitement. He carefully laid her on a towel covering the dirty floor, and opened her legs about thirty degrees for the big finish. Outlaw backed up to the corner of the stage, to get a running start. Full speed, he ran into a forward flip and pounced on top of Ebony, putting his massive manhood in her face as he pretended to satisfy her pulsating treasure, and made the crowd go wild. The dollar bills rained all over them as fans showed their appreciation.

Outlaw pulled Ebony off the hard stage floor, and gave her a thank you kiss on the cheek for being a good sport. She rejoined her jealous friends, who instantly passed her one of a set of shot glasses they all inhaled. Her drunken body fell into an empty seat.

"Now *that* is a wedding present." Ebony pointed back at Outlaw, right before her head landed flat on the table as she passed out.

"That girl's not ready to get married." said Melody, shaking her head.

Chapter Two

Waking up on her 800 count white cotton sheets the morning after her bachelorette party, Ebony realized today was the day she'd dreamt of for the last twenty-five years. The aroma of white lilies and pink orchids would fill the grand ballroom of the Embassy Suites hotel. All fifteen tables would be set up symmetrically with white lace table cloths for the 3 o'clock reception. One hundred and twenty-five friends and family members would witness the union of Ebony Lovely to Carson Brody.

At the age of six, Ebony had her wedding day planned out with her Barbie and Ken dolls. She knew that one day, the love of her life would come and realize the fairy tale she'd always wanted.

A single ray of sunshine broke through the window, warming her face to wake her. Sitting up in her queen sized bed to wipe the sleep from her eyes, Ebony felt a chill come over her, as she noticed she's completely naked. To add a bigger shock, out of the corner of her eye, she saw a figure sharing the left side of her bed. Still half-drunk from the night before, Ebony tried to remember why her fiancé would be in her bed the morning of their wedding. She peeked over the top of the covers to reveal a *bald head* and realized that wasn't her man. Ebony screamed, leaping from her bed, ripping the sheets off to cover herself, knocking her lamp of her night stand.

The stranger rolled off the bed and hit the cold wooden floor with a thud.

She peeked over the bed. "Get out! Get out!"

The stranger jumped up and ran around to gather his clothes spread across the floor.

"What are you doing in my house?!" Ebony screamed. The same naked man that spun her ass in the air last night was dashing naked around her bedroom.

He climbed into his fruit of the looms and crumpled blue jeans on the floor.

"I had a great time last night. Can I call you sometime?"

Ebony picked up her gold heel that lay on the side of the bed and threw it at the stripper's head.

"Ouch, shit!" She nicked the top of his head as he ran towards the door, holding his forehead. The door slammed shut behind him. Her body slumped to the floor, as she tried hard to remember what happened the night before to lead her to this morning. Ebony made a promise to herself that if Carson ever proposed, the cheating would stop, and she would devote herself to being a good wife.

Ebony noticed the clock flashing in the background. "The power must have gone out . . ."

Needing to know the time, she crawled off the floor to find her cell phone, when a knock came from the front door. She scurried to the door, pulled it wide open and exposed herself.

"Eww, put some clothes on."

She ran back down the hall to her bedroom. After managing to find a long t-shirt to put on, she returned to the door, to her best friend, Melody.

"Girl! What happened to you?" Melody observed the disorder of her friend's usually tidy apartment. "First I see a half naked, sexy ass man running out of your building, and now you look like death warmed over. This is turning out to be a crazy morning."

"I can see that."

"You *do* know that it's ten o'clock and we're supposed to leave for the church in an hour?"

Ebony let out a holler. She hopped across the cold kitchen floor to put on coffee. As she stared at the coffee maker, watching the black liquid drip into the pot, an image came into her head.

She remembered a group of half a dozen girlfriends sitting around a wooden table, watching men take all their clothes off, and planting dollar bills down several g-strings. The memory of her bachelorette party came back to her. But Ebony didn't remember leaving with a stripper . . . but how did he end up in her bed? And what did she actually *do* with him?

She poured her coffee, and thought. *Do I tell Carson about my mysterious morning and risk losing him forever, or do I keep this secret and start my marriage off with a lie?* Carson made it very clear there'd be no last-night flings on *either* part before the big day. She knew Carson probably sat around at a bar with the fellas last night and talked shit, but that clearly wasn't what she had in mind for her last night of freedom.

An hour later, her tiny one bedroom apartment was filled by her sister and her mother. The four ladies had to head to the church and get ready. Melody grabbed the dress hanging on Ebony's closet door, as her sister India grabbed the makeup bag and a small case filled with a change of clothes for the reception. They raided her sister's refrigerator. India was one of those skinny people who could eat all day and gain no weight.

"Is that everything?" asked her mother. She surveyed the room for any left-behind items. No-one responded. "Ebony, is that everything??" Her daughter suffered from stress overload.

"Mom please, my head is killing me."

"No-one told you to get drunk last night."

A loud series of beeps came from the street as the limo driver pulled up.

"Aren't they supposed to call us, not honk? That's ghetto." India stuffed an apple slice into her mouth.

"Let's just go, Mom!" Ebony loved her mother to death, but her parents could be very hard on her. The four ladies rushed out of the house with wraps on their heads, and stepped into the white stretch-limo that waited to take them to the church.

Ebony took a seat by the window, riding backwards. She stared out the rear window and watched her apartment building fade away as the limo sped off. She'd been so preoccupied with the wedding plans that she hadn't even packed up her apartment. She was due to move out at the end of the month, only seven days away. Since they weren't going on a honeymoon, she'd have time to get things in order.

Melody sat opposite her and stared into her brown eyes trying to get a read on her. "Cold feet?" An uneasy smile came across the bride's face as she continued to look out the window.

"You could *act* happy, this is supposed to be the best day of your life!" Mrs. Lovely nagged. Ebony gave her mother an evil look. The last thing she needed was to hear her mother's mouth.

The driver stopped in front of the church and opened the car door. Melody grabbed Ebony's arm before they entered the old brick church.

"What is going on with you?"

". . . Nothing." Ebony's right eye twitched, as it always did when she lied.

"So you're gonna look me in my face and lie. I know you better than you know yourself. So spill."

She looked around to make sure no-one was in earshot. "The man you saw in the hall this morning came out of *my place,* and I don't know what happened with him last night. All I know is I woke up naked. Smelling of sex." Melody covered her mouth with her hands in disbelief, almost dropping the dress, and started laughing hysterically.

"It's not funny!" Ebony playfully pushed her best friend. "How drunk was I??"

"Obviously more than you let on. So was it good?" Ebony gave her a sarcastic look as she turned her back. Melody took the hint and left her friend with her thoughts. Ebony turned to face the church, took a deep breath, standing for a minute looking at the church and all it stood for. She let out her breath slowly, thinking of the life she was leaving behind, and the new one lying ahead. She shook her head and let the thought disappear.

Feeling the pressure of time, the four women hurried to get dressed. Mrs. Lovely wore an elegant cream-colored pants suit, while her bridesmaids wore light pink strapless dresses that extended all the way to their French manicured toes in 1-inch heels. Simple yet classy.

"You look beautiful . . ." Small droplets welled in the corner of Mrs. Lovely's eyes as she gazed at her daughter, in her long pure white strapless dress, with lace covering the skirt of the dress and a 12 inch train to follow her. Ebony stared at herself in the mirror, trying to get her thoughts together. Her palms were sweating, as well as her back. Nervousness, excitement, and anticipation all hit her at once.

As Ebony stood at the back of the church, arm in arm with her father, her legs felt like lead. She felt she couldn't walk down the aisle. Her father's lips gently graced the top of her forehead.

Her introduction music called her as the congregation stood to welcome her. Mr. Lovely put his left foot out to walk, and Ebony grabbed his arm back. She closed her eyes, tilting her head toward Heaven, wishing she could see her grandmother to ask for guidance. One by one, she took three, huge, slow breaths. She opened her eyes, and fixated on what was in front of her: her future. She squeezed her father's hand. She was ready.

Ebony took the first step, and her father followed his little girl.

Unable to get the betrayal out of her head, Ebony walked slowly down the aisle, looking to the man she'd loved for twenty years, ever since his family moved next door to hers. Her father proudly handed her over to his future son-in-law and smiled in approval. She returned the smile and kissed her father gently on the cheek.

Ebony looked around the church at all the colorful guests with their big faces, bright smiles, and big hats. As she looked to her future husband, all she could think of was all the sexy men she'd be giving up, and the one she had last night. Although she had no memory of her one-night stand, she'd still miss it all.

Her eyes drifted over to the five groomsmen off to the Reverend's left. She admired all the men with their creased black suits, fuchsia vests, and fresh shape-ups. She smiled at the men, and knew she did an excellent job picking out their outfits.

"Do you, Ebony Yvette Lovely, take this man to be your lawfully wedded husband, to have and to hold and blah, blah, blah?"

She felt like a character in a Charlie Brown cartoon, trying to decipher the minister's words. She felt her makeup start to run. Her hands were already sweating, and she tried to let some air come between her hands and Carson's.

"Ebony?" The reverend repeated.

"Yes sir?" Ebony lifted her head.

"I asked if you take this man to be your husband?"

Ebony turned to Carson. Anger was spilling across his face. He could feel her hand pulling away, but he tightened his grip. She blushed in embarrassment. Her mind wasn't on their wedding, and she hoped no-one else could see the struggle she and her fiancé had on their hands.

"*I do.*" She smiled and squeezed Carson's hand reassuringly. He returned the smile out of courtesy, but still wasn't happy with his blushing bride.

After the ceremony, the couple stayed behind at the church for pictures before heading to their reception. "Who is that strange bald-headed man who sat in the second row? He wasn't on the guest list."

She knew that tall, dark, and bald had always been her type. The camera bulbs flashed.

"Oh, that's Jefferson, someone I knew in college. It's a long story."

The photographer gave them a forced smile. "Say cheese!"

The Brody's arrived at the reception. The wedding coordinator announced her as Mrs. Carson Brody for the first time. She smiled at the thought of having a new name, and sad at the same time of losing her own.

The rest of the wedding day went along as only a dream wedding could. The guests enjoyed themselves. The stuffed chicken, rice, and vegetables were delicious. The bride and groom danced the night away, wrapped up in each others arms. Everyone held their liquor, so there were no embarrassing moments from drunken family members.

About midnight, the reception wound down and the couple retired to their honeymoon suite at the hotel. Ebony hadn't yet found her calling in life. By day, she answered phones at her mother's doctor's office, and at night, she worked part-time as a waitress. Carson was a copy editor for a small publishing house. The two decided to forgo a honeymoon to save money.

Carson swept Ebony off her feet as he carried her into the master suite. "Are you ready for a night of wild, passionate lovemaking?"

She wrapped her manicured hand around the back of his neck. "I'm *always* ready for you."

Carson carried his new wife into the gigantic bedroom and laid her down on the king-size bed. A little out of breath, he sat next to his wife and admired her beauty.

"This feels like a dream to me. I can't believe I married you."

Ebony smiled. "Well believe it, because this is one dream we should never wake up from."

Ebony rose from the bed to take off her beautiful—but uncomfortable—wedding gown. (She never did change clothes for the reception.) She went to slip on the silk nightgown she picked out six months ago, just for this special night.

"Do you really mean that?" Carson hollered from the other room.

Ebony peeked her head out of the bathroom.

"You know how much I love you, don't you?"

"I do, but at the altar; you scared me when you hesitated. I know we've had our issues in the past . . ." She slipped back into the bathroom, not wanting to bring up her mistakes from the past again.

"That wasn't about you. I just had a moment."

"What kind of moment?" She stepped out of the bathroom in a lacey nightgown, exposing her perky nipples; her black hair flowing down her bare back.

"Wow!" Carson forgot all about their discussion.

"Let's not talk . . . How about we try something *new* tonight?"

Carson sat up in the bed. "Okay, I'm intrigued."

Ebony strolled over to her husband. After Carson had proposed, he and Ebony made a pact not to have sex again until their wedding night . . . which had been a very long nine months.

"I'm glad we waited. It makes this moment so special."

Ebony shook her head. "I'm tired of waiting. I need you right now."

Carson stood, taking her delicate body in his arms. He turned the radio to a soft jazz station, setting the mood. The two of them danced one last time before consummating their marriage. As they danced, Carson breathed in the smell of her apricot bodywash and ran his fingers down the middle of her back, making her shiver.

He kissed her right shoulder as he slipped the nightgown off her. Working his way down to her exposed breast, he licked one

9

slowly, playing around her nipple. She grabbed him in excitement, feeling the pleasure she'd missed (from him) these last nine months. Carson lifted her slight body up as Ebony wrapped her legs around his waist, holding onto him. Still not letting go of her nipple, he walked to the edge of the bed, placing her on the edge.

He peeled his bride, letting her nightgown fall to the floor. Her body shivered as the cool air touched it. Ebony slid her body to the top of the bed as Carson smiled eagerly. He climbed on top of her and continued to pleasure her with his tongue. As he made his way down her body, she held her breath, hoping that night would be the night that he pleasured her fully. For some reason, Carson wouldn't perform oral sex on her, and she didn't know why.

Carson made his way to her baby toe, and still no pleasure like she anticipated. She opened her legs slightly, hoping he'd take the hint and slip his tongue in between them. Not taking the hint, he continued on his straight path returning to the top of her body, kissing her softly and entering her gently. He made her orgasm twice. But she still didn't get what she so desperately wanted.

⌇⌇⌇⌇

Lying in his arms, Ebony thought back on the last nine months. All the planning she'd done . . . for a few hours' enjoyment. She stared at the new jewelry on her finger, hopefully for the rest of her life. The ring represented their continuous love that couldn't be broken. She thought back to a time in the fifth grade, when Carson had given her a blue ring pop and promised her that one day she'd wear the real thing. She laughed at him as she licked the lollipop, never thinking one day she'd really be wearing his diamond ring.

Her thoughts kept her awake. Ebony feared that her wild ways impacted their relationship once again. He'd been her friend since they were little. No judgments. Just full support and her husband deserved the best.

Chapter Three

The warmth from the New York sun in Mid July came shining through the hotel window, where Mr. and Mrs. Carson Brody lay in each others arms.

Starting as friends, Ebony and Carson met when his family moved into her neighborhood when he was five. They were arch-enemies from the start, which bloomed into puppy love. Dating all through high school and college, she was his best friend, and he was hers.

On the night of their college graduation from NYU, the two families got together to celebrate. Carson stood up halfway through desert to make an announcement.

Tapping his fork against his water glass he demanded attention from the table full of friends and family members.

"May I have your attention please?"

"Sit down big bro," Carson's sixteen-year-old sister fussed. He cleared his throat.

"I want to say something. I just want to thank both my parents, and Dr. Alberta and Mr. Ron, for supporting Ebony and me over the years as we became the fine, well-educated individuals we're today."

Ebony raised her glass. "I second that."

"And so," he continued, "as we move to the next stage in our lives, I hope we'll take that journey together. And hopefully . . ." Carson moved from his seat to the other side of the table, to Ebony. "Hopefully, she'll continue by my side, and do it honorably . . . as my wife." Carson went to one knee and pulled out a little black box holding a shining 1½ carat diamond ring. Ooohs and aaahs went around the table and the restaurant, as everyone admired the ring. All eyes were on Ebony as everyone awaited her answer.

A smile came over her face, revealing a dimple on her right cheek. She shook her head slowly (and with a little twitch of her eye) she whispered the word yes. She leaned down to kiss Carson . . . which she'd never done in front of her parents before.

"Well, it looks like we need some champagne!" Mr. Lovely went to find the waitress. Carson slid the ring on Ebony's shaking finger and returned back to his seat. Ebony's caramel skin was bright red as she stared in admiration at the rock on her finger. Applause came from other patrons in the restaurant.

Melody, sitting beside Ebony, grabbed her hand to get a closer look.

"Girl! That is some ring."

"It's beautiful."

"You ready for this?" Melody whispered.

Ebony looked down at her ring, then along the table to Carson's best friend . . . whom she'd been sleeping with.

"I guess."

Ebony was a little shocked by the proposal; she thought the plan was for the two of them to get set into their careers before they made any big moves. Marriage was the biggest move of all.

Ebony couldn't imagine settling down with any other man. She knew deep down that no-one could provide for her like Carson could. Even though he was her total opposite when it came to sex and relationships, but the truth was she needed someone sane like him to help her grow up.

The couple recently bought a large two bedroom townhouse with 1½ baths, a fireplace, and a small deck on the west side of White Plains New York.

She suggested getting a house in the city, but Carson knew that wasn't wise for them as newlyweds. Carson was a level headed man, which Ebony had always admired. She was a free spirit and frequently made rash decisions.

Chapter Four

Every Wednesday, Carson played basketball in a league for older men, and Ebony was there to support him. The Wednesday after their wedding was no different. The big day was over, and life was back to normal. Carson and a group of middle-aged men got together for some exercise and it was one of the few things that really made him happy.

Ebony attended the game with her best friend Melody, a lover of basketball and men. They watched the thirty-something-year-old men interacting as if they were dancing. The girls giggles at the round bellies jumping up and down and the men over forty were gasping for air as they ran up and down the court. Being one of the youngest guys in the group, Cason was still in really good shape.

Melody nudged Ebony's shoulder and pointed down the court. "Who is that?" Ebony followed her finger towards the only other man on the court in shape. She tried not to check out men with her husband around.

"I don't know."

"Wasn't he at the wedding?" Ebony stared a little harder, recognizing the man guarding Carson.

"Yes!"

Her mouth fell open in disbelief. She couldn't believe her eyes. The same fine stranger that showed up at her wedding had re-entered her world. "That's him."

"He is fiiiine. I'm going to get that."

Ebony ignored her horny friend and focused her attention back on the bald stranger. She imagined herself as the little droplets of sweat forming on his body. He took his shirt off and used it as a towel to wipe his face. He exposed his rippled abs and muscles, flexing every time he moved. Ebony stared, daydreaming about cleaning his sweaty body with her tongue.

"Baby?" Carson called out as he and Jefferson approached.

"I want to introduce you to somebody. This is my boy Jefferson."

"Yes, I saw him at the wedding. I was curious how you ended up there, when I know I didn't send you an invitation," she said slyly.

Jefferson smiled.

"It's really a funny story, because he just moved back in town, and happened to be at the same place as my bachelor party. I told him I was getting married, so I invited him."

Ebony reached out and Jefferson took her hand, shaking it ever so gently, thinking her husband was too damn nice.

Melody cleared her throat, demanding some attention. Ebony took the hint.

"This is my best friend Melody."

Jefferson licked his lips, took her hand, and kissed the top of it.

"Hello, best friend Melody. My pleasure, I'm sure." Melody blushed as the men ran back onto the court to finish the game.

"What do you think of him?" asked Ebony.

"I think he's delicious, that's what I think."

Ebony laughed. Melody always had dick on the brain.

"I mean, I've never seen him before, then he shows up at Carson's bachelor party, our wedding, now basketball. That's weird, isn't it?"

"Well, Sherlock, let me know what you find out, and I'll let you know what I discover."

Ebony rolls her eyes. After the game, Melody ran over to Jefferson and forced her card into his hand, not taking no for an answer. Ebony watched her best friend's hand linger on his.

Flashing back to high school and feeling a little jealous of Melody, Ebony remembered how her best friend always got the attention of the finest men, while she sat on the sidelines wishing it were her. In this case, she hoped Melody and Jefferson never hooked up.

Chapter Five

Ebony called her best friend bright and early to make sure she kept her word. "Are you still going to help me pack up, today?"

"Huh, what?" She could tell her best friend was still in the bed. Ebony raised her voice to shake her out of her dream.

"MELODY!"

"What! I hear you girl, give me an hour, and I got you."

Two hours later, Melody strolled through the apartment door in big round sunglasses and a baseball cap, to find Ebony taping up boxes and marking them storage, trash, or new home.

Ebony snorted. "You look like crap, girl."

A huge grin came over Melody's face. "That's okay. I *feel* incredible."

Ebony stopped. "Why's that?"

"Cause I got me some good loving last night, the kind that makes your legs shake and all that."

"For real?"

"Yeah girl." Melody gave her a high five.

"Is this a new victim?"

Melody grabbed the tape out of Ebony's hand, and started taping up the open box Ebony had been packing.

"I told you I was going to get him."

"Him who?"

"Jefferson's fine ass."

Ebony stumbled. "What!"

"He called me last night, we met at a little bar to have a few drinks and it was on."

Ebony was taken aback while she listened to her friend recap her escapade with Jefferson. She was trying not to get angry with Melody, but on the other hand, she had no right to feel that way because she had married the man of her dreams.

Ever since childhood, Ebony thought of how many times her best friend had stolen a man away from her. From her very first boyfriend (who Melody hooked up with the night the two of them had broken up), claiming she'd been so drunk that it just happened. While their friendship had always been stronger than any man, the truth was, Ebony knew Melody was easy, loved sex, and as long as Ebony remembered that, she knew what to expect. Carson was the only man Ebony had been with that her best friend had never tried to get at. Melody claimed Carson was just too nice for her.

"Hey sis, how are you?" Carson came through the front door, dangling truck keys. He gave Melody a slight hug. "I got the U-haul. You ready to go?"

"I think so. You can start taking all the boxes that say 'storage'."

"So." Melody sauntered around Carson like a stripper trying to make a dollar. "Tell me about your boy Jefferson."

Carson chuckled to himself. "You trying to get at that?"

"Trying? You know me, a sister got that all ready."

"Really?" Carson sounded shocked.

"Surprised?"

He shrugged. "I don't know, we went to college together for two semesters. Then he disappeared. I'd never seen him with a lady except one. In fact, some of us questioned which way he swung."

"You're kidding!" Ebony couldn't believe a man that fine could be gay.

"I don't know. He was always a strange character. That's all."

"Then why invite him to our wedding?"

Ebony knew that answer before she asked the question. Carson was the kindest man she knew. He'd give a stranger his last dollar if he felt the person really needed it.

"He just happened to be there that night, and we were talking about the wedding in front of him, so I had to invite him."

"Okay, too much detail," said Melody. "Can we get this moving thing over with? 'Cause a girl's got things to do today."

The three of them finished moving Ebony's things out in two hours. Ebony stayed to clean up, while Carson took her things to the new house, the dump, and a small storage space her parents had rented for her. When she was done, Ebony sat on the floor, reminiscing about all the memories she'd created there. She closed the door behind her, putting an end to her single life.

Chapter Six

All the wedding gifts were put away, and all the thank you notes finally written. The wedding commotion had subsided, and it is back to work as normal. Ebony found herself back at her little desk, answering phones and listening to other people's problems all day long, through the intercom in her mom's office. Looking out the small window of her office at the hustle and bustle below, she wondered if she'd find her true calling and stop working herself to death.

Samantha Gray, one of Ebony's favorite clients, walked in for her ten o'clock appointment. She was a successful criminal lawyer who had a problem. She loved sex, and might even be an addict.

"Hello, Ms. Gray. What juicy story do you have for me today?" Every time she came, Samantha told Ebony some torrid affair she was having. Ebony *loved* the gossip.

"I did it again. This man was perfect though, the marrying type. He's in advertising and *sexy as hell*. Like Billy Dee back in the day."

Ebony chuckled, remembering how cool he was in *Lady Sings the Blues*. "We met one night at a party for the mayor, and the attraction was instantaneous. I took him back to my place and we had wild, crazy sex that was *amazing*. I was walking funny the next morning, you know what I mean?"

Ebony laughed hard. She knew exactly what Samantha was talking about.

"Don't stop, go on!"

"So anyway, this man keeps calling me because he wants to take me out and see where this thing can go, but I can't bring myself to call him! And then the next day, I slept with one of my clients. I'm so ashamed."

"Why the client?"

"He is on trial for 1st degree murder, but I think he's innocent. But he had that . . . *badness* about him, and his deep voice and his thug attire; he just *exudes* sexiness. He's the kind you just want him to turn you over and spank you so hard that—"

Ebony covered her ears. "TMI! I get the point." She took a sip of water. "I told you, you have commitment issues. See there, I just saved you a bunch of money. Maybe *I* should be a therapist."

Dr. Lovely came out of her office. "Samantha, I'm ready for you."

Ebony waved at the lawyer. "See you next time!" Samantha winked in return.

Five o'clock came quickly. Ebony headed off to the restaurant for part two of her day.

"Hey girl!" She waved at Janice, another waitress, as she tied on her apron.

"When are you going to quit this job?" asked Janice. "Now that you're married, your husband should be taking care of you."

"Ttch. In a perfect world, maybe." Ebony laughed as she clocks in.

The hostess yelled to Ebony. "You got a table."

Ebony walked into the dining room. "It's show time."

Walking up on her table, she saw a tall, bald man with his back sitting to her. Her heart skipped a beat at the thought of the man sitting in her section.

"Fancy seeing you here, Jefferson."

"A man's gotta eat. I know my body's perfect, but I do love a good steak. And I didn't know you worked here." Jefferson smiled, but somehow Ebony didn't buy it.

"Are you dining alone?"

Jefferson showed his pretty white teeth. "Just me. Are you going to serve me?"

Ebony blushed, seeing through his flirtation, but she enjoyed the attention. She took his order, then leaned over him to grab the menu from off the table. Jefferson brushed his hand against her arm, making the little hairs stand up. She pulled her hand back, hoping it was an accident, and ran off to the kitchen.

Later, as Ebony left his bill on the table, Jefferson asked her to join him.

"I can't sit, my boss will see me."

"Will you go out with me?"

Ebony blinked. "Weren't you *just* at my wedding?"

"You can't have friends?" That smile hit her again.

"I have friends, thank you."

Jefferson looked at the bill, pulled out some cash, then handed the book to Ebony. "Sometimes it pays to have friends in high places."

He got up and walked out of the restaurant. Ebony looked inside the book and saw $200 . . . and his business card. Her mouth dropped open, realizing he'd left her $125 for a tip.

Chapter Seven

The Merritt Athletic Club opened every morning at five in the morning. Carson made it a point to be there by six for his workout. Being on the slender side, Carson was trying to build up his upper body so he had the muscles he knew Ebony loved.

Because of the wedding, it had been almost three weeks since he'd been to the gym. He dropped his bag in the locker room and headed for the treadmill closest to the TV that played Sports Center. He plugged in his earphones, but put them around his neck when his boy and Best Man Michael walked up.

"What's up, bro?"

He stepped down off the machine to hug him. "Chilling, chilling."

"So how's married life?" Michael stepped onto the machine next to him.

"It's good, man. I mean, I've been with Ebony so long, I thought it'd feel like we're still dating, but it's different. I know she's all mine forever, and the fact that there *is* a Mrs. Carson Brody . . ." He shook his head. "Man, I love it."

He started out in a slight jog.

"You sound like it! It was a nice ceremony, and that bachelor party was a good time."

Carson and Michael both took a moment to reflect on Precious, Candy, and Delicious—exotic dancers at the party.

"So you cool with having the same woman for the rest of your life?"

Thinking of all the sex Ebony had been giving him lately, Carson nodded his head.

The two of them moved onto the weight room. Carson loaded 120 pounds on the bar and laid down as Michael stood to spot him. He did a set of ten bench presses and sat up to rest.

"Looking good over there," said a tall slender woman, from across the room. She set down her free weights, swung her weave over her shoulder, and walked over. "It's been a while," said Leslie, happy to see him.

Carson sized her up. "You look *good*." Her biceps were forming up nicely.

"So do you. I heard you got married, I guess I should say congratulations."

Carson took her sarcasm with a grain of salt. "Thanks."

Leslie had flirted with Carson for years, and made it known she thought she was a better woman for him than Ebony. Back in college, the two of them hooked up one night at a party, and the guilt had been weighing on Carson ever since. Ebony had never found out about his betrayal and he wanted to keep it that way. Carson had forgotten about that night 'til six months ago, when Leslie randomly joined his gym a month after he did. This was the one and only secret he'd ever kept from his wife.

The two men watched her walk away. Michael shook his head. "Man, if I were you, I'd grab her, take her into that locker room, and let her feel what she had been missing."

Carson dismissed it. "I don't want her. She's fine, built, and bootylicious, but she's *no* Ebony."

Michael nudged Carson off the bench and laid down to do his sets. "*I'd* still hit that ass one more time."

"You know her and Ebony were friends until Leslie stole her crush at the time. That was before we hooked up though."

Michael chuckled, remembering the two women rolling around on the ground, fighting back in high school.

"Women are scandalous."

Chapter Eight

Ebony checked herself out in the mirror, before standing. "I'm going to the store honey, do you need anything?"

"I need you to come over here and sit on daddy's lap so we can make some babies." Carson walked to Ebony and grabbed her by the waist to kiss all over her. She looked at him like he'd lost his mind.

"You know that is not *even* a topic of conversation."

"Fine!" He shook off his agitation. "Just some deodorant please. Want me to come?"

"No, keep your horny ass in the house."

"Hurry back, so you can take care of this." He pointed down to the bulge in his pants. She laughed and ran out the house.

Ebony was mad at herself for not shopping earlier, so now she was forced to deal with all the slow Sunday drivers. Ebony jumped into her silver Honda Accord and sped off down the street towards the super market. Instead of taking the direct route down the highway, she basked in the beautiful sunny day and drove along back roads.

Ebony pulled her car into the Safeway parking lot and parked. She sat there, digging in her purse for her wallet to make sure she had enough cash with her. Fumbling through her purse, a little card fell to the floor of the car. Ebony leaned over to get it, realizing it was *Jefferson's* card. He'd been on her mind a *lot* lately. The way he kissed her hand made her feel very hot inside. She was curious if all the details Melody gave her about their passionate night together had been true.

For no explicable reason, she picked up her cell phone and dialed the number, not knowing what she'd say. The phone rang three times before the machine picked up. She let out a sigh of relief as she hit the end button on her phone. Before she could put the phone away, it started vibrating in her hand. After a moment's hesitation, Ebony hit the talk button on the phone.

"Someone just call Jefferson?" His sexy voice says.

"Hi . . . It's Ebony."

"So, to what do I owe the pleasure of your call?"

She stutters, knowing there *was* no good reason to call him. "I—I wanted to thank you for the tip, but I can't accept it. So I need to return the money."

"Girl, please. That was for your exceptional service." She could envision his slick smile on the other end of the phone.

"So I see you have my number. Make sure you use it again." The phone went silent, and Ebony realized he had her number, too . . . in more ways then one.

Chapter Nine

The telephone rang just as Ebony stepped into the house with an armful of groceries.

"Hey girl, what you doing?" Ebony recognized Melody's voice right away. She made her way to the kitchen and started banging some pots around.

"Just about to make dinner!"

"Well stop what you're doing, because you need to get dressed!" Ebony was too tired for Melody's brand of excitement.

"Dressed for what?"

"You know that guy I started dating? Well, he's having a party tonight at some club, and I want you to come with me."

Ebony stood at the ceramic kitchen sink staring out of the little window that sat above it. "It's a Sunday, I have work tomorrow."

"Come on, we haven't been out since the wedding! Bring Carson if you want!"

She sunk down over the sink, knowing Carson wouldn't do anything unless it was planned out a week in advance at least.

"You know how Carson is! Besides, he thinks no married woman should be in a club because she's attracting the wrong attention."

Ebony stood straight up to get a bottle of water from the fridge. She *hadn't* been out for a good time with her friends since her bachelorette party. Now she really wanted to go, but she knew she needed to take care of her husband. If she didn't fix him dinner, he might go hungry tonight.

"Let me fix dinner first, then I'll let you know."

"Ebony . . ." Melody whined, upset.

Ebony noticed a piece of paper taped to the fridge: a note from Carson. He had to run back to the office to get something and wouldn't be back for an hour. After a quick moment of contemplation, she decided to have some fun and deal with the consequences later.

She put a sexy black and white wrap around a dress that tied on her left hip, a long silver necklace that reached her navel, and a pair of black sandals. She ran out the door.

The club was a little spot on the corner of 8th street and Lexington. Ebony had passed the spot many times because it was close to her mom's office, but she'd never stepped foot into the club before tonight. As she entered, all eyes turned in her direction. She held her head high, smiling at all the haters, then searched the room for her best friend. The bar was the first thing that caught her eye.

To her left was a large area with colored couches and big bright pillows for people to relax on. Straight back was a small dance floor with a silver disco ball spinning in the middle. This was very much Ebony's scene. She loved the 70's style. She glimpsed a flashy gold shirt and some too-tight black pants on a woman, and knew it was Melody shaking it up on the dance floor. Ebony waved at her to get her attention.

"Hey girl, you just get here? You look good!" She leaned in to hug her. "See? I *told* you you needed to get out of that house!"

Ebony cocked a stubborn hip. "So *since* you dragged me out, making my husband mad at me, you need to buy me a drink."

"No prob!" Melody walked towards a tall, full-figured brown-skinned man, leaning against the bar and entertaining a small group of men.

"Baby, I want you to meet Ebony." The man turned around, extending his hand to greet Ebony. Her new man Kevin, the birthday boy, ordered the girls two cosmopolitans and resumed his conversation.

Ebony sipped on the drink so it wouldn't spill over. "This place is nice. You've been here before?"

Melody nodded. "Kevin brought me here once, but that's it."

Ebony glanced back towards the bar checking out her friend's new man as the ladies settle into a mauve-colored couch with burgundy pillows. "So tell me about him!"

Melody smiled at the thought of her new man. "Well, it's still early, but he's cool. We have a lot of fun together and the sex is good, so I'll keep him 'til he pisses me off."

"They always do . . .", They took another sip, and Ebony slid back into the couch to get comfortable.

Melody looked concerned. "Is Carson really mad about tonight?"

"He'll be fine . . . Oh my gosh." Ebony sat back up and stared down. She spotted Jefferson eyeing her up from the middle of the dance floor. She smiled slightly and raised her glass to say hello. He gave a slight nod to make his presence felt, then returned to his dance with a skinny model. Ebony was instantly jealous.

"What are you doing?" asked Melody. "Seems that man is just following you around the city." Ebony smiled, partially liking that thought.

"You want him don't you." Melody laughed, bouncing up and down on the couch.

Ebony smacked her on the arm. "Stop, you're making a scene! Oh, I don't deserve Carson. I'm a terrible person . . ."

Melody waved away her friend's concern. "Girl please, you wouldn't be human if you didn't have thoughts about other men, it's natural!"

Ebony finished her drink in one gulp. "I need another drink."

After two more Cosmo's, all of Ebony's morals had flown out the door. She was up on the dance floor, two-stepping with her best friend.

Jackson stepped between Ebony and Melody, grabbing Ebony's hands as the song slowed down. "Mind if I step in?" Freddie Jackson's *You are My Lady* blasted out of the speakers. Jefferson pulled her close, feeling her hips against his. His body rocked from side to side, whispering in her ear. She closed her eyes to take in the smell of his cologne as she wrapped her hands tighter around his back.

"That's it, hold on to me," he whispered, making her forget that a diamond ring sat on her left ring finger. She resisted a little, feeling too comfortable in his arms. He felt her weakness and pulled her back in, kissing her softly below her ear. Ebony pulled away quickly and ran off toward the bathrooms. Jefferson watched her scurry off, rubbing his hands together, knowing it was just a matter of time before his plan comes full circle.

Once she was alone, she stared at herself in the mirror, looking for answers. Ebony ran her fingers down the side of her neck. The wetness from his kiss still lingered long after his lips were gone.

"What is *wrong* with me?" She couldn't figure out why she wanted Jefferson so much. She had already betrayed her husband in her thoughts. Could Jefferson push her back into her wild, cheating days?

Chapter Ten

Carson received the message that he would have to get his own dinner that night, because his wife had gone out with Melody. He was instantly bothered. He wasn't fond of Melody; he knew what a freak she was, and didn't want his wife hanging out with single women and getting pushed back into her old lifestyle.

Carson was an old-school guy who liked home-cooked meals, and his woman staying at home, raising children. He'd never fully discussed this with Ebony, because he knew how career-oriented she was.

A starving, irritated Carson now had to find something to eat and there was only one place that he would go: Sylvia's. It was as close to home-cooking as he could find, and it was near his job, which was even better. He entered the restaurant, planning to take dinner home. From there, he'd sit in front of the TV, watching *Sixty Minutes* or whatever news program he could find. But once he was in the restaurant, Carson realized he didn't want to be alone. So he settled for *eating* alone, surrounded by strangers.

He smiled at the attractive young hostess that greeted him. "Table for one?" She showed him to a small booth in the corner, opened the menu for him, smiled, and let him know his server would be right with him. Engrossed in the menu, Carson didn't notice Leslie's long legs approaching the table until she was directly in front of him.

"Now *why* would a newlywed be eating dinner all by himself?"

He put down the menu. "Leslie, how are you?" He stood to greet her.

"You didn't answer my question . . ." She gave him a sexy, sneaky smile.

"Ebony went out."

"Want some company?"

His head screamed no, but he extended his hand to the empty seat anyway.

He waited until she was seated before he sat again. "Wow, there aren't many men like you left in the world. I hope Ebony knows how lucky she is."

Carson smiled shyly out of embarrassment. He handed his menu over to Leslie, so she could decide what she wanted. He already knew he was having smothered chicken, greens, and macaroni and cheese.

The two of them ordered, and enjoyed an intellectual conversation of politics and crime. A few glasses of red wine later, they both felt a little tipsy, and their talking turned to flirting.

"Can I ask you a question, Carson?"

"Did you not enjoy me when we were together, all those years ago?"

Carson chokes on his chicken. This was the one topic he never wanted brought up again.

"Can I be honest? This will never go beyond this table?"

Leslie nodded. "That's all I want from you. Honesty."

Carson took a deep breath, hoping it was the wine talking.

"I enjoyed our night together very much. Actually a little *too* much. I've always been in love with Ebony . . . and when you paid attention to me, I don't know. It spun my head. But it was a fluke.

I'm not that guy. I would never step out on Ebony." He finished his glass.

"But you *did*."

"I know. And I have to live with that for the rest of my life."

Leslie ran a finger around lip of her glass. "Do you regret it?"

There was a pause.

"No."

She smiled as if she had won the grand prize.

The waitress approached, breaking up the eye contact between the two. "Can I get you some dessert?"

"Um yes, I'd like a piece of sweet potato pie."

"That sounds good, make that two." A look of disbelief fell over Carson's face.

"What?" Leslie asked. "I'll just have to put in a little extra time at the gym tomorrow."

Carson paid for the meal like a gentleman. Leslie tried to leave the tip, but he didn't allow that either.

"This was really nice. I'm glad I ran into you tonight. You saved me from having dinner alone."

Leslie reciprocated with a nod. "Thank *you* for dinner. Any time your wife leaves you for the night, just let me know."

Leslie leaned in and gave Carson a light kiss on the cheek, and a hug. He walked her to her car, before heading home, hoping to find the woman he loved.

Chapter Eleven

Usually, the Brody household was early to rise, except this particular Monday, where both husband and wife were trying to sleep off mild hangovers. The alarm clock was silenced for the first time at 5:30AM. Ebony rolled over to stare at the little red numbers, seeing it was now 8:30AM.

She wiped her eyes to clear her vision. Not too worried about the time since her first patient wasn't due in until 10AM, she snuggled back into bed for a few more minutes of sleep until she heard snoring behind her.

"Carson, do you know what time it is?" She nudged her husband.

"What? Stop pushing me."

"It's 8:30 already."

"Okay." He was nonchalant, until the words sunk in. "Oh shit!" He leapt up from the bed. "How could you let me oversleep? Now my whole day is going to be ruined, my whole routine is off for the day." Ebony sat up, watching her control freak husband run around the room reprimanding himself.

"I should just stay in bed. A million things are going to go wrong today."

Ebony laid back on her pillow, giggling to herself. "Why don't you come back to bed and wake up all over again? You need to calm down before you make yourself sick!"

As a child, Carson used to have bad panic attacks from trying to be so perfect all the time. It had gotten better with time, but he still felt sick if he got worked up too quickly.

"You know this is your fault," he said, sliding his pants up over his behind.

"How is it my fault?" she asked, offended.

"If you'd stayed home last night, I wouldn't have had to eat out and drink three glasses of wine and I would've gotten up on time this morning."

Ebony sat up again. "I can't believe you're blaming me. Whatever you did last night had nothing to do with me. You could have come straight home and done your same boring routine, Ate dinner, watched the news for half an hour, take a shower and do your crossword puzzle before you turn into bed at ten."

Carson stopped buttoning up his shirt. "Are you making fun of me?"

"Not at all," she growled, "but excuse me for not wanting to do the same thing day in and day out for the next fifty years. It's called living, you should try it sometime!" She didn't realize she'd started yelling until she was done. Carson grabbed a tie and a pair of black shoes, and left the bedroom, irritated.

"Don't forget to shine your shoes!"

She heard the front door slam. Ebony ran to the bedroom window and watched Carson speed off down the street. *He had some nerve,* she thought, *blaming me for him going out and drinking too much.* Then it dawned on her that Carson *never* drank with dinner. He hardly ever drank unless he was socializing. She reached for the cordless phone sitting on the night stand, about to dial his cell phone to find out just exactly what he did last night . . . but something stopped her. She had no room to question him, because she hadn't been an angel herself.

The phone started blinking in the palm of her hand. The caller ID read Melody so she answered it.

"What's up chica? Just called to see how you are this morning. Was Carson mad about last night? You can blame it all on me."

Ebony walked to the mirror to finish getting dressed. "No, it's cool. I have a bit of a headache, but I'll live."

"I'm glad you came out."

"Yeah, me too. I gotta run, Melody, I have to be at work by ten."

"How bout lunch?"

"That'll work, just come by the office."

Ebony hung up the phone and made the bed. She saw Carson's clothes laying on the floor, so she picked up his pants to put them in the hamper. A small piece of paper fell to the floor: a receipt from Sylvia's for seventy-five dollars. Having a woman's intuition, she ran down stairs to check the refrigerator, hoping he'd brought her home some food last night. Nothing. Her first instinct was to call her husband and find out what he actually ate for seventy-five dollars, but her gut told her he wasn't alone last night.

As Ebony drove to work, she was thankful for being late because there was no traffic. Ebony arrived at the office in record time. Her mother is in Ebony's seat, answering the phone. She gives her a dirty look.

"I am so sorry mom, I had a rough morning."

"Carson already called, saying you'd be late." Ebony turned her face up. He had no right to call her mother.

"What else did he say?"

"You just need to get yourself together. Carson is the best thing to happen to you. Get it together."

Ebony stared in disbelief. She'd never heard her mother talk like that. Her mother stormed off into her office, shutting the door. Ebony took her seat, looking over the appointment book.

Ebony showed a fifty-something woman into the office. "Can I get you anything, Mrs. Harper?"

"I'm fine dear, thanks."

Ebony pulled out a small note pad and looked the words she'd written. She started to play around with the words, composing a song. Ebony had always loved music. Like most little girls, she loved singing, and wanted to be a singer when she grew up. The difference was, she had real talent. Her parents never let her pursue her dream because they wanted a stable career for their daughter.

Standing up from the uncomfortable chair, she walked around the empty waiting room with the notebook still in hand. She started singing her song out loud, arranging the words to make sense. She leaned against a warm windowpane, letting the sun beat on her face. She became louder as the song started to come together.

"Your eyes tell me things that your mouth could never . . ." She imagined she was performing in front of an audience. Being in her own little world, Ebony didn't hear the office door open. She got up from the window and began to dance around, using a pen for a microphone. She twirled around dancing, until she hit a high note and opened her eyes.

"Oh shit!" There was Jefferson, leaning against the doorway. He started to applaud.

"Please! Don't stop on my account."

Her brown skin turned a shade of bright red. "I thought I was alone."

He made his way into the office. "You sound great, ever thought about going pro?"

"No, I was just fooling around . . ." She sank her head in embarrassment.

"So did you enjoy yourself last night? 'Cause I sure did." He sat his fine ass on the side of her desk.

"It was okay."

"Why didn't your husband join you last night?"

"He . . . doesn't like to go out."

Jefferson chuckles to himself.

"What?"

"Let me tell you something." Jefferson pointed his finger at her and stood up, taking a step towards her. "If you were *my* woman, I wouldn't let you go out alone."

Ebony gave a hmph. *Glad I'm not your woman, then,* she thought. The man didn't hesitate. "Go out with me."

She turns to walk away from him. "Have you forgotten a little ceremony you attended a few months ago, called my wedding?"

"I remember." The minty scent of Listerine passes by her nose and she realizes how close Jefferson is standing.

"Please, just go out with me once. I want to take you someplace nice."

She turned quickly to face her enemy. "And what about my husband? I'm just supposed to tell him I have a date??"

"Tell him you're working late at the restaurant. You're smart, you'll think of something." Jefferson reached up, rubbing his hand against her cheek. She closed her eyes, becoming excited by his touch. He wets his lips and kisses her neck.

"Tomorrow at 8. I'll pick you up from here." And just that quickly, he was gone. Her legs felt weak, and they buckled from under her. She collapsed to the floor. Less than a minute later, Melody walked into the office to find her sitting cross-legged in a brand new Donna Karen pants suit.

"Girl, get off the ground. What is wrong with you?" Melody walked up and started tugging at her like she was a child.

Ebony stared at her with a dazed look in her eyes. "I love my husband. I really do . . ."

"Okay . . ." Melody patted her head likes she was crazy. "No-one's questioning your love for Carson."

"Then why am I hot for another man?"

Melody started to laugh, until she realized Ebony wasn't joking.

"Oh Lord." Melody flopped onto the floor with her. "This is a talk we need to have over a drink".

Chapter Twelve

At seven o'clock, the last client left, and her mother followed right behind her. Ebony was the only one left in the building. She looked herself over in the mirror, touching up her makeup, thinking how ridiculous she was being. She was waiting to go on a date with someone other than her husband.

"No. I can't go, this is insane." Ebony went to her desk phone to call Jefferson and cancel. Just as her finger touched the first number, she felt Jackson's presence in the doorway.

"You ready?"

She took in a long breath, and let it out slowly. With his fine physique standing in front of her, she lost all nerve to cancel. "Not really."

She clicked the lights off and locked up the office. The two of them climbed into Jackson's black Lexus and raced off into the city.

"If I know anyone at this spot you're taking me, then we're just colleagues going out after work." Jefferson nodded in agreement, knowing that none of Carson's uptight friends would be there. During the rest of the ride, they didn't say much. Ebony's nerves had the best of her; she had nothing intelligent to say. Every so often she feels Jefferson steal a peak at her and a small smirk comes over his face.

The car finally stopped at a spot she'd never been to before. It was a little hole in the wall with pink awning and a florescent light in the window. She knew she never would've noticed at this place.

Once inside, an older black man greeted them and showed them to a little table in the corner, with a small candle on the table.

"This is *funky*." Ebony took her seat on the little wire chair with a padded seat.

Jefferson sat opposite her. "I like it, it's different".

"So how did you find this place?"

"Actually, I play here." Jefferson waved to the band onstage.

"Play what?"

"You'll find out." He gave her a winning smile. Ebony smiled, enjoying the mystery that was Jefferson.

The same older man got up on stage, getting the audience's attention. "Ladies and gentleman, I'd like to start this set off with one of our favorites . . . If Sly will join us on stage, we can begin."

The audience applauded and shouted out in approval. Ebony searched the room, trying to figure out who Sly was, until she noticed everyone looking in her direction. Jefferson stood up to take a little bow. He walked up to the stage and grabbed the microphone.

"Thanks pops. I actually can't do a set tonight . . ." The crowd started to boo. "Unless a lovely lady would accompany me with some lyrics." Jefferson extended his arm in Ebony's direction, and a small spotlight shone on her. She blushed in embarrassment, scared out of her mind. But . . . she'd always wanted this opportunity. She slowly rose from her seat, shaking her head at Jefferson.

The stage was black as Ebony stepped into the light, with a smile that demanded attention. A hush fell over the crowd. She wrapped her manicured fingers around the microphone, and held it like her lover. She looked to her left at Jefferson, holding his guitar. She gave him a nod and he started playing an old Anita Baker song. She closed her eyes as the words started to flow from her.

Ebony opened her eyes and saw the smiles of approval in the audience. She turned back to look at Jefferson, in his own grove. Her skin glistened from droplets of perspiration. Ebony felt the song coming to an end, and she prayed her voice would hold out to finish the song off right. She finished flawlessly. The crowd was on its feet. Ebony exhaled as Jefferson grabbed her hand, and took a bow with her. She gave his hand a squeeze, thanking him for letting her live her dream.

After the set, they lingered, listening to the other musicians. Ebony, still on her own adrenaline high, leaned across the small table and kissed Jefferson on the cheek to thank him. She loved places like this, but she knew that Carson would never be caught dead here. At that moment, something hit her. She knew she loved her husband, but a part of her wondered what things they really had in common.

Once the evening came to an end and the club started to clear out, Jefferson exchanged goodbyes with the band. He coaxed Ebony to join him by the stage.

"You need to bring this pretty lady back so she can sing with us again".

Ebony smiled, blushing.

They headed back to Jefferson's car. On the ride back to her office, she stared out the window with a huge grin on her face. She'd never felt so alive inside. She hadn't felt this good since college, when she sang at open-mic nights.

They finally arrived back at her office. Ebony checked the parking lot before slipping out of the car and running into the building. Something told her to go up to the office before she headed home.

"Mrs. Brody." Ralph the night watchmen startled Ebony as she ran to the elevator.

"Oh, Ralph! You scared me!" She stopped suddenly, as if she had just been caught sneaking into the house like a teenager.

"Sorry ma'am, I just wanted to let you know your husband was here about an hour ago, looking for you with a big picnic basket. I know a few women who'd love to be in your shoes!"

She smiled uneasily, feeling guilty. "Thanks, Ralph. I appreciate you telling me."

"Sure thing, ma'am. Have a good night."

"You too."

Ebony made a u-turn from the elevator and headed straight for her car. She felt absolutely horrible. Carson was such a sweet man and would never suspect her of doing wrong, and she knew she *was* terribly wrong. The worst part was, she had to lie to her husband . . . and one lie always led to another.

Chapter Thirteen

BANG! BANG! BANG!

Melody ran to the door, snatching it open.

"What are you, the damn police? And what are you doing here at this time of night?"

Ebony pushed her way into the apartment and flopped on her best friend's couch.

A tall, naked man walked out from the bedroom. "Babe, what's going on?"

"Oh shit." Ebony covered her eyes quickly as the man strutted around, swinging his manhood.

"Do you mind??" Melody swats him away.

"What is wrong?" She joins her friend on the couch.

"I can't go home. I lied to Carson and he came by the office looking for me and *what am I doing* . . . Why didn't you talk me out of getting married? I'm not ready to give up my wild ways!"

Melody stopped her. "Hold up! Start over. What did you lie about? And where were you?"

Ebony took a few long breaths. ". . . I went to a spot with Jefferson tonight, and I had so much fun. I feel so alive and I want this man so bad, but I'm married now and my cheating days are over. What do I do?"

Ebony buried her head in the cushions. Melody stared at her, not quite sure what to say. She patted her friend on the shoulder, opened her mouth, then closed it. She did this several times.

"I don't know what to say."

Ebony looked at her with tear-drenched eyes.

"Tell Carson that *we* were together, and get your butt home. It's late."

Ebony picked herself up, wiping her face. She walked to the door, when Melody stopped her.

"If you really do love Carson, you need to stop whatever this is before it starts. I know it's hard to commit to one person, but you have to *try now* get some sleep. We have a party tomorrow."

Ebony grabbed her best friend, hugging her tight. Then she ran out the door.

By the time Ebony pulls into the driveway, it was almost midnight. Driving home she sent Melody a text saying that if anyone asked, the two of them had a late dinner and she had caught a ride with Melody and left her car parked at work.

She crept into the house, trying not to wake Carson. She noticed the picnic basket, sitting on the kitchen counter . . . untouched. She looked inside to find a bottle of her favorite wine and carry-out from the Olive Garden. Ebony unpacked the basket before going up to bed.

As soon as the covers were un-tucked, Carson woke up. He grabbed her by the waist and pulled her close to him.

"Where have you been??"

"I'm sorry, you should have told me you were coming by."

"I went by your restaurant but you weren't there, so I figured you were at your mom's office."

She kept her back towards him the whole time so she didn't have to lie to his face.

"I did, and then Melody stopped by and we went to get something to eat. I'm sorry the time just got carried away from us."

Carson's grip tightened around Ebony's waist as he began to rub down her thigh and kiss her shoulder.

"I just feel distance between us lately, and I hate it."

"How 'bout we spend some quality time together and make love all night? I'll even do that thing you want me to do?" Ebony's face lit up like it was Christmas.

"What?"

Carson shrugged. "How bout we please each other . . . together."

Ebony's face lit up even more. She could never get Carson to give her oral sex and now he wanted to sixty-nine.

Carson rolled on top of her and made his way in, using his finger to satisfy her at the same time. Carson started to make love to her and Ebony was totally confused. Ebony wanted her husband to taste her most private place, but she knew he'd never do that. She asked him once in college, and he said that his father always told him that men shouldn't use their tongues for that. At which point, Ebony knew why Carson's mother always looked so unhappy.

Ebony made no comment. She just closed her eyes and let Carson have his way with her, until he rolled off her and fell asleep a minute later. In a way, she felt relieved. Now she didn't have to get on top for round two.

She rolled over, looking at the smile on Carson's face as he slept. Ebony couldn't sleep a wink. All she could think about was Jefferson and how much she yearned for his strong hands to caress her body, and those luscious lips to kiss her breasts. Her body started to moisten as the thoughts become more real. Ebony started making little moans, and her hands started moving up and down her body . . . then she did something she'd never done before. She pleasured herself, and to her surprise, it was more satisfying than what she'd just had with her husband.

Ebony knew her feelings for Jefferson were going too far. She had to put a stop to all of this.

Chapter Fourteen

Carson's thirtieth birthday had arrived. Ebony had planned a small surprise party for him at the house. She hoped the get-together would help put some stability back in their marriage. She had invited his family of course and a few mutual friends they have and left the rest of the guest list up to Michael. It was a Saturday, and Michael agreed to keep Carson out of the house for the whole day, doing 'guy things'. She'd told everyone to arrive promptly at 6PM to give the guests an hour before the boys arrived. At 5PM, the girl team knocked at Ebony's door.

Ebony had macaroni and cheese baking in the oven, she'd made potato salad and prepared a vegetable tray when Melody and India arrive with more food and decorations.

"Hey sis!" India walked in carrying a huge tray of 100 buffalo wings and Melody followed with a sandwich tray.

"You two are the best!" Ebony kissed them both on the cheek before taking what they'd brought.

"The cake's in the car, I'll grab it." India ran back out.

Melody pulled her coat off and hung it in the hall closet. "Do you think he suspects anything?"

Ebony shook her head. "No. Things have been kind of rough lately, and I just want to make it up to him. You know how he hates surprises."

"It's a shame, 'cause he's almost a perfect package. Smart, sexy, got a good head on his shoulders, and a *positive* brother. He just needs some adventure in his life."

"If he wasn't afraid of giving oral sex, I'd have to fight women off him with a stick."

Melody shook her head, about to laugh, until she saw the real pain in Ebony's face.

India come back in the house with a full sheet cake in her hands. "Just what are we talking about?"

"Grown folks business", said Melody. She and Ebony shared a look and started to laugh.

"Any cute, single men coming tonight?" India asked, hopping up on a wooden bar stool by the island in the kitchen.

Ebony shook her head. "I left the invitations up to Michael, so I don't know."

"Great. That means he invited all his immature friends."

"Is your new man coming?" Ebony asked Melody.

Melody gave a nod. "He said he'll be here."

By quarter to seven, the quaint townhouse was decorated and three quarters the way full of guests, mingling and on their first round of drinks. Ebony changed into a simple but sexy black dress, and a pair of one-inch heels. Ten minutes to seven, Michael texted her and said they'd be pulling up in five minutes.

Ebony ran through the house. "They're coming! They're coming!"

All the guests gathered in the foyer. Ebony dimmed the lights as they waited. Melody was standing directly in front of the door, ready to catch Carson's reaction at the moment of his surprise. The key jingled in the door, and Ebony pulled it the rest of the way as everyone jumped out and yelled surprise.

Carson's face became bright red with embarrassment, although he wasn't the only one getting a surprise. Ebony's jaw dropped as *Jefferson* walked through the door right behind Carson and Michael. Melody shot Ebony a look of disbelief as Ebony shrugged back at her.

Carson leaned in and kissed his wife. "I'm going to get you for this . . ." She returned the kiss, and pulled back to spot Jefferson staring her dead in the eye. Her smile disappeared.

"Excuse me!" Ebony excused herself to mingle and make sure everyone was having a good time.

"Cover me." India came up behind her sister. "Who's that loser with the glasses over there in the plaid buttoned shirt?"

"I think he's Carson's cousin."

"He's following me around, talking about "you must have fell from Heaven cause You're an angel". What is *with* these eighth grade lines?"

They both laughed and went their separate ways. Ebony made her way to the kitchen for a drink. A glass of wine didn't seem strong enough, so Ebony made herself a jack and coke. It wasn't very ladylike, but she didn't care. Plus, if Carson wanted some tonight, she needed to be a little tipsy.

"I'll have what you're having."

She looked up into a pair of clear brown eyes she'd come to loathe—only because they belonged to a man she wanted, but couldn't have.

"It's just a jack and coke."

"It's a man's drink. I like a woman who can take a real drink."

Ebony looked him dead in his eyes, took a long gulp, and slammed the empty glass on the counter. She gave him a sinister smile and walked out of the kitchen. Turned on, Jefferson followed. As she made her rounds around the house, checking the parts of the house that were suppose to be off limits, she reached the coat closet. In an instant, Jefferson grabbed her arm, pulling her into a dark room not being used by guests.

"*What are you doing??*" Ebony shook her arm free.

"I needed to talk to you, and you haven't called."

"I said everything I needed to the other day. I feel horrible that I went out with you!" she whispered.

"You had a good time. That smile on your face when you were singing was priceless." Jefferson touches Ebony's arm and pulls her closer. He started to whisper in her ear, as Carson walked pass the room, noticing their intimacy. Ebony caught his shadow out of the corner of her eye, and wondered what he was thinking. His sensible side would shake it off as nothing, but his other half would wonder if there was something to worry about. Carson slipped back around the corner.

"This is neither the place nor the time. I can't *believe* you're even here!" Jefferson moved in and kissed her on her neck, before she quickly pulled away. Ebony scurried out the room and around the corner, and tried to blend in. India saw her sister joining the group late.

"Help me get the cake," asked Ebony. India followed her to the kitchen and grabbed some candles from the top drawer.

"I don't know what you're doing, but you need to stop. Now."

Ebony ignored her sister as always, and lit the candles. It wasn't long before everyone was singing.

As Carson cut the cake and served out slices, Melody leaned in towards her best friend.

"What was that about?" she whispered.

Ebony tried to shoo her away. "Sshhh, I don't know. He said he needed to talk."

"About what?"

"Not now."

Jefferson broke the conversation. "I must be going, ladies." He smiled devilishly, and walked out the door, but not before giving Carson a wink and a devilish smile. Carson's brown skin immediately turned red in anger.

Melody and Ebony looked at each other confused. Melody shook her head in disappointment. Ebony rolled her eyes in return, and walked away. Ebony excused herself from the party and made her way upstairs to the bedroom.

She went to the bedroom windows facing the front of the house and watched Jefferson walk to his car. He turned to look, feeling her eyes on him. winked. She didn't return the gesture.

Her thoughts were getting the best of her. She had to find a way to get Jefferson out of her head for good. Ebony slumped to the ground and started to cry into her hands. She knew what a good thing she had going with Carson, and didn't want to hurt him, or lose her security.

After splashing some water on her face, she rejoined the party, standing by her husband for the rest of the night. Once all the guest had left, Ebony looked around at the mess.

"Thank you for the party." Carson kissed her on top of her head. "I'm exhausted." Ebony smiled at her husband as he went up to bed. Five minutes later she heard his snoring, and knew he was in a deep sleep.

She put on a pot of coffee. She picked up trash. She swept the floor and put away the leftovers. Once hazelnut aroma filled the air, Ebony took a long sip and crashed on the couch.

Chapter Fifteen

C arson came down the steps in an especially good mood, while Ebony was exhausted from a restless sleep. "Good morning, sweetie. How did you sleep?" He kissed her on the forehead, avoiding her morning breath.

"I'm on the couch, what do you think."

Not ready to get up, she turned over, putting her face into the cushions to block the sunlight coming through the window.

Carson poured himself some coffee. "How 'bout I take you to lunch? I have to go to the office for a while, but after that?"

"I can't," said Ebony, "I have some business to take care of today."

"Anything special?"

She thought for a minute. She really had nothing to do. She just wanted to be alone to clear her head.

"No, just some stuff."

❧

Forcing herself to get up, Ebony did her hair and makeup before she got in the shower. It was backwards from her normal routine, but she could feel it was going to be a backwards kind of day.

She grabbed a pair of wrinkled jeans and a white t-shirt and hopped in her car. She drove to the hole in the wall Jefferson had shown her. Ebony grabbed a little two-seater table off in the corner, and sat alone with her sorrows. After her third drink, the betrayal of her actions consumed her every thought. But with every impure thought of Jefferson came one of significant pleasure. She couldn't figure out when her own pleasure had been put before the pleasures of her husbands . . . or their marriage.

"Hey there young lady, you going to bless us with that voice of your tonight?"

The nice older man who seemed to run the place had interrupted her thoughts. She thought for a minute, not feeling like giving a performance, but also needing an out-of-body experience. So she decided to join the stage one more time.

She sang like her life depended on it . . . and in a way, she felt like her marriage *did*. Every feeling she'd trapped inside came out in her singing. After she belted out her last note, she hung her head in exhaustion. The small crowd went wild. Her eyes were filled with tears as she took a small bow for her fans and returned to her seat.

A small gentleman dressed in jeans and an un-tucked button-up shirt came over to Ebony's table. "Nice song, young lady. You do this for fun or are you serious?"

"No, I just enjoy messing around, is all." She took one long gulp and finished her drink.

The man cocked his head. "Shame. If you ever get serious, give me a call." He placed his card on the table and walked away. Ebony lifted the card, not knowing what to feel. She thought about herself as a little girl, singing into her Barbie dolls, pretending they were microphones. She and India had even put on a concert for the neighborhood when they were about eleven. Singing was the one thing that brought her peace.

The small black card seemed to stare at her as she rose up from her seat, ready to leave. Ebony walked away from the table, leaving her dreams behind. She took five steps before she returned to the table, scooped up the card, and stuffed it into her purse. She returned home a little before 8PM, to find her husband watching the news and eating Chinese take-out. Ebony walked right by him and finished cleaning up the mess from his birthday party.

Chapter Sixteen

Carson sat down on his wife's side of the bed, waking her up. "We need to talk." She knew it was coming, but not at 1AM.

"What about?" Ebony shifted slightly to reposition herself for whatever was coming.

"Us, babe. What's going on with us? We feel . . . broken, and I hate this. Is it because we've been together so long? Have you fallen out of love with me already?"

Ebony's eye twitched. She felt a lie coming on, but stopped herself. Yes, she loved him and always would. But was she still *in* love with him? That was the big question.

"I love you, Carson. I always have. It's just . . . things have changed."

Carson shifted uneasily on the bed. "What do you mean 'changed'? And what was that talk between you and Jefferson about last night?"

"Baby, don't take this the wrong way, but our life had been *boring* since we got married. We didn't get a honeymoon, and that's fine, but we haven't done anything *fun*! We just went on with our same lives, and I feel that you want me home all the time, and frankly, it's kind of *dull*."

Carson swallows hard. "Okay, so what do you want to do to make life more exciting?"

She sat there, pondering the right things to say, but the only things she could think of were to be more spontaneous and adventurous . . . But Carson couldn't really change his ways.

"I don't know. I *do* know that I don't have any passion or drive inside me anymore, and it's killing me."

Carson blinked, taking this in. "And Jefferson?"

"He just said that the party was nice, and asked about India, that's all."

Carson took a knee in front of his wife, and took her hand in his. He put his head in her lap and started crying. Ebony lightly touched the top of his head, confused about where the tears were coming from.

"What is wrong?"

"Just know that I'm sorry." Carson picked his head up and walked away.

Ebony sat there in disbelief. Yes, the marriage was a little rough right now, but she had never seen him react like that. Ebony didn't follow her husband, she let him go. Her mind started to wander. Did Carson have a secret of his own to hide, to make him react like that? And what does he have to be sorry for? She stretched out in the bed, agonizing over how she *still* couldn't be totally honest with the man who stole her heart. She wanted him to know she really *had* been thinking seriously about singing. Being on the stage in front of people was the one thing that truly made her happy and free . . . and if she didn't go for it, she'd feel trapped forever.

Carson came back looking refreshed. He moved to the bed, leaned in and gives her a deep kiss. The kiss led to the two of them writhing on the floor, and making love like the night they got married.

"I do truly love you, Carson." Ebony looked up into his eyes, hoping he'd see the truth.

"I love you too, baby." Carson met her lips again, and they made love a second time. The couple fell asleep in each others arms on the floor.

When the sun rose, Ebony woke with a newfound look on her marriage. She realized she needed to make it *work* and leave Jefferson *alone*. Her cell phone rang, and Jefferson texted her about how much he wanted to see her. She had no idea why he was so insistent.

Chapter Seventeen

S ince the beginning of his existence, Carson had dreamt of a woman of such beauty, grace, confidence, and independence as Ebony. Carson worshipped her, and he wanted her to know it. So much so that he planned to surprise her with a special evening to rekindle that love that seemed to be slipping away.

His Thursday morning started off like any other. Waking up at 5:30AM to hit the gym by six, shower and shave, grab his coffee, then head off to the office to be in by eight.

Before checking his messages or opening the pile of mail from the past two days, Carson turned on his computer. Determined to close the distance he was feeling from his wife, Carson ordered a dozen mixed roses, and sent them to his wife with a note: "I love you and can't wait to see you tonight."

Carson leaned back in his leather chair and smiled, anticipating the incredible night ahead. His thoughts were to hold her in his arms and make love to her like they used to. They hadn't been married a year, yet their sex life had dwindled almost to the point of extinction.

By two o'clock, Carson managed to wrap up his day and was ready to head out for the ingredients he needed to make the only dish he could cook well: stuffed shrimp.

He pulled up to their town home a little past 3:45PM, still fuming, but trying to put it aside to have a pleasant evening with his wife. Ebony usually got home by half past five, so he had ample time to get the house in order. Ebony hadn't been taking care of the house; laundry is overflowed onto the floor, and the kitchen table was covered with mail and newspapers a week old.

Carson began to straighten up, setting up candles as he went. He went to Ebony's personal stash of scented candles and displayed them on any free counter space or ledge that he could find. Before starting dinner, he took a shower and changed into a pair of slacks and a polo shirt.

By quarter after five, everything was in place for his beautiful wife. Dinner was just about ready: A beautiful Caesar salad on small plates, a perfectly aged red wine open and breathing, and Carson standing at the door with two wine glasses, ready to sweep her off her feet. He grinned like a little kid with his first crush . . . for the first fifteen minutes. Then he pulled up a bar stool and sat with a half smile, for the next twenty-five. An hour later, Carson had moved to the couch after three glasses of wine.

Getting worried, he called Ebony's phone, which went straight to voicemail. He tried her at the office, which got no answer either. By seven thirty, Carson had gone through every emotion: anxiety, sadness, worry, anger. Something told him to look on the refrigerator door at Ebony's schedule at the restaurant. She wasn't scheduled to work. He rubbed his head, wondering what was keeping her. He finally decided to turn in.

Across town at the office, Ebony sat in a state of confusion, between two men. She'd received the flowers and shot him an email, thanking him. Carson never mentioned he had anything special planned for the evening. Since she was in no rush to get home, Ebony decided she needed some time away to clear her head.

Ebony peeked her head into the suite of Dr. Richards, the psychiatrist that shared the office with her mother. "Doctor, I need your help."

"Ebony, come on in."

"You busy?"

"Not at all." Ebony walked into her office, and sat on her chaise lounge.

"So it's one of *those* conversations." The doctor pushed away from her desk, and moved over to her little brown chair by the chaise. "You need to talk?"

"Can I talk freely?" Ebony looked up with desperation in her eyes. Dr. Richards knew it was serious. She closed the door and returned to her seat.

"So what's on your mind?"

Ebony took a deep breath in and exhaled slowly. "Please don't tell my mother any of this." The doctor nodded. "You know I'm recently married, but I'm . . . *drawn* to this other man that is so different from my husband. He's spontaneous, sexy, and he drives me crazy inside! I don't know what to do. At first I felt horrible, then I felt good, and now I feel bad again, but I'm starting to feel something for this man . . . and I have no idea what to do."

Ebony exhaled again. For the next half hour, Ebony told Dr. Richards about her life with Carson, and what she felt was missing from their relationship, and how she lusted for another man.

∽⊷⊱⊰∾

By the time Ebony pulled up to the house, it was a quarter past nine. She walked into the quiet house and was surprised. *Carson never goes to bed this early*, she thought. An empty wine bottle sat on the counter, and the house smelled of burnt candle wax. Her heart dropped as she realized Carson had tried to surprise her with a romantic night. As she crept into the bedroom, she stood in the doorway, watching Carson sleep. She walked over to his side of the bed and gave him a soft kiss on the forehead.

"I'm sorry," she whispered. She climbed into her side of the bed. Carson opened his eyes and looked at her.

Chapter Eighteen

The next morning, Carson didn't feel like going to the gym, which wasn't like him at all. He lay in bed, unable to get up. The distance in his marriage was killing him and he couldn't take it. They weren't suppose to be like this.

He rolled over to touch his wife, but she was nowhere to be seen. He reached for his cell phone. As he dialed her number, Ebony walked into the room in her running shoes and exercise clothes.

"You went for a jog?"

"Yeah!" She mopped sweat from her forehead. "I just needed to clear my head. And why didn't you tell me you had a dinner planned last night? I wouldn't have stayed late at the office!"

"It was supposed to be a surprise. I guess we just weren't on the same page." He sat upright in the bed.

"I'm sorry! I really wished you would've told me."

Carson looked in her eyes, wondering what secret she was hiding.

"Let's have dinner tonight. We need to spend more time together."

"I have to work tonight, but I'll take a rain check?"

Ebony crossed to him and gave him a reassuring kiss before she jumped into the shower to start her day.

❦

As Ebony maneuvered through the morning traffic, the only thing on her mind was the long day ahead. She thought that if she kept her days busy enough, her mind wouldn't wander to Jefferson. At this point in her life, she needed him to be a distant memory.

"Morning, mom." She smiled warmly as she entered the office. "Any coffee?"

Dr. Lovely looked at her skeptically. "Isn't that what I pay you for?"

Ebony gives her a little smirk. "I'll get it." She started thinking about getting a job away from family.

Ebony poured herself a cup of coffee with lots of cream. She hardly ever drank coffee, unless she had a lot on her mind.

As she settled into her desk, the appointment book read Samantha Gray, at 10AM. She always looked forward to Samantha's visits.

Ms. Gray rushed in at the last minute, like always. She comes right up to the desk with a smile on her face like she just had the best time of her life.

"I'm in love, I swear I am soooo in love this time."

Ebony tries to hide her smirk, but she just didn't get how a powerful attorney could get so excited over dick.

"What convict is it this time? A murder, a rapist, what?"

"Girl, I am *offended*. I'd never do a rapist, I have standards. But seriously, he's the district attorney, and I swear I've never seen a finer man in my *life*."

"And the sex?"

"We haven't done it yet. See, it's not even *about* that. It's different this time . . . it's about so much *more*."

63

Ebony listened to Samantha go on about the man, and secretly hoped her relationship wouldn't last, because that would be the end of her wild stories.

Samantha gave Ebony a genuine hug before she went in to talk to the doctor. The minute her waiting room was quiet again, Ebony leaned back in her plastic chair, closed her eyes, and took a long breath. In, and out. She opened her eyes to her cell phone beeping. A text message popped up from Jackson, reading "Hello sexy, just thinking about you."

Ebony deleted the message instantly. Before she knew it, her day had come to a close and she hurried into rush hour traffic to get to her second job on time.

Ebony greeted her boss as she ran into the kitchen, putting her things down. "Hey, sorry I'm late."

"Katie called out sick today, so I need you to close."

"Great! Let me text my husband so he won't wait up."

By midnight, Ebony's feet were throbbing. Ebony looked in her pocket at the mass of her tips. "Good night . . ." She says to herself. As she wrapped up all the trash from the dining room, she dropped the bag by the front door and waited for the manager to let her out, and lock the door behind her.

"I'll dump the trash."

"Okay, be careful." Her manager waved as he watched her walk to the dumpster. She threw the bag in and slammed shut the lid.

"Oh, shit!" She jumped back as she saw a figure standing in front of her. Then she recognized him. "Are you stalking me, Jefferson?"

"You got my calls?"

"I did. And as you see, I didn't respond."

"That's unwise." Ebony backed away from the dumpster, feeling uneasy.

"Why are you fighting this? I just want to show you what you're missing." Jefferson kept pressing her back, until she bumped into the brick wall.

Jefferson wore a t-shirt that read Florida A&M, and a pair of baggy green sweatpants that looked atrocious, but they filled his lower half out well.

Jefferson looked intently at her. "I need to talk to you."

"Now, I know these meetings haven't been by chance. But I want to tell you that they need to stop. I'm a married woman—a *faithful* woman, so you need to stay away from me."

Jefferson stepped closer, her pinning her against the wall. The smell of his cologne drove her crazy.

"Well if you love your husband so much, why's it bother you to be around *me*? I heard you haven't always been such a good girl . . ."

He moved even closer. His breath grazed her cheeks.

"Who—who told you that?" She had nowhere to move.

"Wouldn't *you* like to know." A sneaky smile crept over his face. "It's eating you up inside. You want me so bad and you can't stand it."

"I uh . . . I . . ." She couldn't think of a response. At least none that made any sense. "I . . . should be going."

She tried to make her way around him, but his muscular body was stopping her. The one little street light was giving off little light to the alley way. She was wondering of anyone can actually see them if they walk by.

Her breathing became heavy, looking for an escape. Jefferson stepped in even closer, diminishing the two inch gap between them. With one quick move, he grabbed her waist, lifting her up around his waist to kiss her fiercely. His hands slid up the back of her neck into her scalp, and he slowly lowered her down until her feet were back on the ground. With little resistance, she obeyed his physical direction. She wanted him right then and there, no matter the cost.

His hands loosened her pants, and they fell to her ankles. He gently but forcefully pinned her hands against the wall. She had no control.

The two made eye contact and no more words were necessary. Jefferson slid himself down in a kneeling position and pleasured her body like no-one had before. Ebony moaned and groaned, never once thinking of her husband, never once trying to stop the pleasure.

After her body trembled with a complete released, Jefferson joined her in standing.

"There's plenty more where that came from." In a split second, he was gone. She took a moment to catch her breath before pulling up her pants, and running off to her car.

"DAMN, DAMN, DAMN!"

Ebony beat on her steering wheel, furious with herself. Her reflection in the rearview mirror turned her stomach. The old, promiscuous, irresponsible party girl she used to be was staring her down. Was it fair to marry Carson, thinking that would change who she was inside? As she was scolding herself, a slight grin came across her face, relishing the incredible sensations Jefferson gave her. Never in her life had she had a lover like that.

Chapter Nineteen

The next evening, Carson surprised Ebony by taking her to *Samba*, an upscale restaurant that highlighted local talent on any given night. It wasn't usually Carson's type of scene, but he knew his wife would love it.

They arrived at quarter past seven. A young light-skinned woman sat them at a private table for two off to the side of the main stage. A small jazz band had set up their equipment and was about to start their first session.

"Good evening, my name is Kiana, and I'll be serving you tonight. What can I get you to drink?"

"I'll take an apple martini." Ebony opened the menu.

"I'll have a glass of merlot, and a glass of water please." Carson replies.

Ebony looked at him with big eyes. He hardly ever drank, and especially not on a work night.

"I feel the need to relax, is that all right with you?" Ebony didn't respond, but turned her attention towards the stage instead, as an older balding gentleman picked up her favorite instrument and started to play. The saxophone relaxed the mood until a man approached the table.

"Hey sweetie, did you come to sing tonight?" Ebony looked up, seeming to recognize the older man standing in front of her.

Her cheeks blushed as she politely declined the offer. He leaned in and gave Ebony a kiss on the cheek, and shook Carson's hand before walking away. Carson's eyes burned a hole in her, waiting for an explanation, but she ignored his stare and continued to watch the band. The server returned with the drinks, and the couple placed their order.

"So you're not going to tell me who that man was?" Carson questioned her.

"I went to a karaoke bar one night and he heard me sing, that's all."

Ebony's shoulders relaxed as their dinner arrived. As she took the first bite of her steak, she looked through the crowded restaurant to spot Jefferson sitting no more than ten feet away with a seductively dressed woman. Carson felt eyes on the back of his head.

Clink went her fork, hitting her plate.

"Hello? Are you with me?" Carson tapped on the table as Ebony stared off in space.

"Sorry, what did you say?"

He leaned in closer. "*What* is going on with you? Where are you right now?"

Ebony pointed across the room at Jefferson's table. "Isn't that your friend Jefferson? Let's go say hi."

Ebony got up from the table and started marching her way across the room before Carson could stop her, so he just followed. Halfway across the room, she slowed down, having second thoughts . . . but it was too late to turn back now.

"What's up man?" Jefferson stood up from the table and greeted him with an uncomfortable hand shake.

"You know my wife Ebony?"

Jefferson grabbed her hand and kissed it. "A pleasure as always."

"This is a friend of mine, Lela." Lela extended her hand to shake Carson's, then turned to Ebony, who just stared at her.

"I didn't know you were dating anyone," Ebony pried.

Carson looked at his wife strangely, then turned back to Jefferson and Lela. "Enjoy the rest of your night." He grabbed his wife by the arm and pulled her back to their table.

"What the hell is wrong with you?" Carson asked his wife. "If I didn't know better, I would think you were jealous!"

Ebony shifted in her chair, uncomfortable. "It's just that he slept with Melody a few weeks ago, then asked about my sister. Who does he think he is? He shouldn't mess with the people I care about. That won't happen."

Carson raised his hand, signaling the waitress for the check. "I'm ready to go."

The whole car ride home was silent. It wasn't until they reached the front door of their townhouse that Carson opened his mouth. Ebony headed straight for the bedroom. Carson sat down on the edge of the bed, taking off his shoes as Ebony dressed for bed.

"What the hell's going on with you? We had an incredible night the other night, then every day since had been just *weird*. I don't know what to think!"

Ebony's brown eyes stare in disbelief. She'd never seen Carson so disturbed. Her right eye twitched. "Baby, my heart is yours. Always had been. And it always will be." Carson took her words as truth, not noticing the telltale twitch in her eye. Still, it wasn't an explanation. He exhaled deeply.

"I just . . . need to be alone for a while."

Those were the last words he spoke before putting his shoes back on and leaving the house. Ebony watched the tail lights trail off. She grabbed her cell phone and called Jefferson. His voicemail keeps coming on. All Ebony could think about was if Lela was enjoying the same pleasures *she* did the other day. She ran to her car, pulled out Jefferson's business card for his address, and took off down the street.

At Jefferson's house, she parked down the street. She crept up to the house, peeking in his windows to see if he was still with Lela. His silhouette passed in front of the window as she stepped on a stick, snapping it loudly.

"Sshh!" she scolded herself.

Jefferson was gone. She tried to prop herself up closer to the window to see better.

"Looking for something?"

Ebony jumped with a shriek, turning around to see Jefferson standing with his arms folded.

"I have a friend in the neighborhood and I—"

"Please. I do *not* have 'Stupid' written all over my face." He grabbed Ebony's arm and dragged her into his house before his neighbors saw.

She snatched her hand back. "Let go of me."

"So you want to tell me why you're sneaking around outside my house?"

"I *said* I wasn't sneaking around." She tapped her foot in annoyance. "Where's Lela? Why isn't she here?"

Jefferson laughed at her jealousy.

"So that's what this is about? You don't want to fuck me because you're married, but you do want to dictate who I can and can't sleep with? I don't think so."

He turns and walks to his kitchen pulling out a bottle of water from his refrigerator. There was something about Jefferson that annoyed and excited her at the same time. She knew that she needed to beat her husband home, because she wouldn't be able to explain if he found her missing.

Ebony followed him and smacked the bottle out of his hands, splattering water about the kitchen. Hurting her, he grabbed her wrists and held them in front of her body. Their eyes locked in the heat of passion. He yanked her wrists closer, pulling her to his chest. Their lips connected and Ebony became putty in his hands. He took a step forward, and placed his hands around her size 30 hips.

Bringing his mouth to her body, he wrapped his mouth around her breasts, slowly teasing the tips of them through her dress. Ebony closed her eyes, savoring the moment. Jefferson unzipped the dress, letting it float to the floor. She stepped out of her lace panties, and he propped her up on his breakfast bar. Spreading her legs apart, he placed them on his shoulders for support, and dove in headfirst. Ebony felt his tongue creep up in-between her legs as he tasted her. She flailed her arms around like a drowning swimmer, trying to find something to grab onto. Her pleasure fueled Jefferson's own excitement, and his tongue started moving faster and faster. Ten minutes later, her body couldn't take anymore. She trembled and let out a loud scream.

"You okay?" he asked, laughing as he wiped his lips.

"That. Was. Amazing."

Jefferson's ego was big enough already, and Ebony had boosted it even more with the big smile she wore.

Jefferson laughed. "I could teach your husband how to do that . . ."

He looked down on her, removing a strand of hair from her face and tucking it behind her ear.

Wondering what else this man could do to her body, Ebony's brown eyes looked up into his, wanting him desperately. He nudged down his pants. He slid her limp body to the edge of the counter, and inserted himself into her wetness.

With no thoughts of her husband, she let Jefferson enter the place that was promised only to Carson for the rest of her life. The first stroke made her body tense up, until they got into a rhythm. From there, she let all thoughts fly out of her head. She reveled in all that Jefferson was giving her; to hell with any consequences.

"Jefferson! Oh! Yes, *fuck me*." She yelled louder and louder. He gave her what her body needed for twenty more minutes, until he collapsed right into her. Ebony started laughing. The pleasure she felt was intoxicating. She turned her head, and saw a clock. It was half past midnight.

"Oh shit!" She pushed him off of her, grabbing her clothes off the floor and running out of the house.

"Damn it!" She scolded herself as she jumped into her car. She prayed her husband wasn't home. Her prayers were answered; she pulled up to an empty house. Ebony quickly ran into the house to wash Jefferson's musk off her. The sound of the garage door opening startled her, just as she stepped out of the bathroom. She leapt into bed and pretended to be asleep.

Chapter Twenty

$\mathcal{E}$very six months, the girls got together for a spa day of pampering and relaxation. A day of massages, pedicures, manicures, facials (and a little male-bashing that every woman needed in her life). The ladies sat around in a large open area, reclining in overstuffed leather chairs, soaking their toes in foot spas with green mud masks on their faces. The room created a feeling of such peace with its tropical music and aqua blue walls.

"That massage felt so good! Kim Lee had the strongest hands. If she were a man, *mm*. The things she could do to me". Melody and Ebony both burst out laughing. "You two know I'm right! What more do you need in life besides good sex and a good massage?"

"I know I really need this," said Ebony.

"I know my man had been killing my back so I definitely need this." Melody relaxed into her massage.

Ebony smiled to herself, remembering the incredible sex she'd enjoyed only a few days ago. Her sister caught the grin on her face.

"What's with that smile?"

". . . Nothing."

Melody looks at her best friends twitching eye. "Spill it, bitch." The massage therapist gave her a dirty look.

"Speaking of good sex," said Ebony, unsure if she should spill her little secret, but needing to tell *someone*, "I had some *really* good sex the other day."

India shook her head. "Okay, Mrs. Newlywed, you don't have to brag about you and Carson. Nobody needs to hear that." Melody looked at Ebony, hoping she wasn't about to say what she thought she was.

"It . . . wasn't with Carson," she whispered.

India's jaw dropped open as she peeled the cucumbers from her eyes, and Melody hung her head at her friend's betrayal.

"What?!" India sat up in her chair, taking her feet out of the water. "Spill the juice *now*, hussy."

Ebony blushed, thinking she should have kept her mouth shut.

"I don't know, it just sort of *happened*. First he came to the restaurant, then mom's office. I tried to hold back my feelings, but my old ways overpowered me."

"Who was it?"

Ebony looked around the room to make sure no-one was in earshot. She leaned in and whispered, "Jefferson."

India scrunched her face up, "Who's that?"

Melody looked at India first. "He was that fine bald headed man at the wedding." She turned to Ebony. "I can't believe you! You knew I was after him!"

Ebony looked shocked at her best friend, now claiming to be in love with her new beau, Kevin. "You moved on, remember?"

"That's *scandalous*." India leaned back in her chair with folded arms, angry at her sister.

Melody returned the cucumbers to her eyes, trying to relax again. "So now what?"

"Now *nothing*. It was a mistake, and it won't happen again. I need to put it behind me, and make sure Carson never finds out."

"Easier said then done," India muttered to herself. Ebony shot her sister an evil look.

Chapter Twenty-One

*J*efferson texted Ebony as she left the massage parlor, wanting her to come over. She went . . . against her better judgment. After leaving Jefferson's house, Ebony couldn't help but smile . . .

Until she pulled her car up to her home, when reality set in. She looked at the clock in her car, and realized she'd been there over three hours. To her surprise, Carson's car was parked in the driveway. That was an unwelcome surprise. Ebony went into the house through the side door, trying to be quiet. The house seemed quiet at first glance. She could hear a TV faintly, and figured Carson was in the basement. She pulled her heels off and hurried lightly across the kitchen floor, trying to make it up to the bedroom to get Jefferson's scent off of her. Again.

"Hey baby." Carson stopped her dead in her tracks in the kitchen.

"You startled me!"

"How was your spa day?" Carson went to her to give her a kiss, but she backed up, knowing Jefferson's cologne was probably all over her.

"I have to go to the bathroom first. I'll be right back."

She ran off with a twitch in her eye, desperate to buy time. Ebony had never been one for lying, that was why she'd always gotten caught by her parents. There was the time she skipped school with Melody; her parents asked her about it and she just confessed, because she couldn't come up with a lie. *This* was one secret she planned on keeping.

Carson heard the shower running as he started to head back downstairs to turn off the TV. Ebony hoped Carson doesn't pay any attention to the shower running, because she couldn't answer more questions that she had to. She let the water beat down on her, and thoughts of Jefferson's tongue all over her body filled her head. With thoughts of pleasure came tears of anguish. She sat back on a little ledge in the shower, and started to cry. She cried for stepping out on her marriage, letting her past get the best of her, and betraying the one man who had always loved her. She cried for having made a commitment she wasn't sure she could keep.

Twenty minutes later, after all the tears had gone, Ebony stepped out of the shower to find Carson sitting on the toilet, waiting for her.

"Oh! You scared me. How long have you been sitting there?"

Carson unfolded his arms and grabbed her a towel.

"I want to know why you were crying." He rubbed her arms through the towel, helping to dry her off.

"I just needed a good cry. Women do that sometimes."

She opened the bathroom door and walked straight past him to her closet to grab a pair of jeans and a T-shirt so she could start his dinner.

"Ebony!"

She continued down the steps to the kitchen. Carson followed.

"Baby, what's wrong? I'm getting a weird vibe from you. Is there something we need to talk about?" Ebony dug in the refrigerator for chicken.

"I'm fine."

"Can I help with dinner?" Carson stood there, looking so innocent . . . it broke Ebony's heart. Carson had always been her friend above everything else; he didn't deserve a cheating wife.

That night, Ebony lay in her husband's arms, feeling safe and secure. A life with Carson would always be safe, and she knew that which was partly why she married him. But deep down inside, there was part of her that was *screaming* to be free again. Not just sexually, but a freedom that children had, not having to think about what tomorrow brought—living for the day, playing hard and enjoying every moment of it.

Chapter Twenty-Two

"Mm, morning." Carson rolled over, grabbing his wife from behind and putting his lips on her back. The softness of her skin felt like silk on his. She rolled over to reciprocate.

"What's for breakfast?" Ebony asked, between kisses.

"I really hope it's you." He started kissing down her neck.

"For real, I am hungry."

He rolled his eyes, and rose from the bed. "You're always hungry."

Carson padded to the kitchen, cracked open some eggs, and whisked them in a bowl. As the butter melted in the pan, his cell phone started jumping across the counter as a picture message came through. His jaw went tight as he stared at a photo of his wife being ravaged by a stripper.

"*What is this??*" He held up his phone as his wife entered the kitchen. Ebony grabbed the phone.

"That's . . . that's nothing. That was my bachelorette party. It was all in fun." Ebony laughed remembering the night anew.

He jabbed a finger at her face. "Ebony, you *promised* me."

"I know I did." She grabbed his finger. "I love you." She smiled, kissing the tip of his finger.

Carson's anger faded at once. "I'm such a sucker for you." He leaned in to kiss her when his phone started vibrating again. This time, it was Michael texting him, saying his wife was all over Facebook in photos with a stripper. Carson slammed his phone down in a rage. Ebony read the text as her husband stormed out of the house. She looked down at the eggs, never cooked, just a stirred up mess. Her heart felt the same way.

Carson kept a change of clothes in his gym bag in the car. He drove off to work, and powered through the day. From work, he drove around without a plan. He called his best friend Michael, but he wasn't home. Carson then went to his home away from home: the gym.

There were only a few cars in the parking lot. The night air felt cool, as a slight breeze brushed against his body like hands, cuddling him. He stood before his car, closed his eyes, and enjoyed the peace.

"Fancy seeing you here," said a familiar, feminine voice. He opened his eyes to see Leslie, staring him in the face.

"Don't you have a wife at home, missing you?"

He slammed his car door. "I doubt it." He walked towards the gym.

"Okay . . ." Leslie ran after Carson. She caught him right as he reached the front door to the gym.

"You sure you want to work out? You seem like you need a stiff drink instead. Besides . . . you're wearing khakis and a polo shirt." She hid a smile behind her finger.

Carson looked down at his outfit. He let out an uneasy chuckle, trying to hold back the tears. Leslie positioned her body between the door and Carson's body, focusing on his glistening eyes.

"Let me buy you a drink."

In Leslie's car, they drove down a back alley to a little country bar where they were the only two black people in sight. The bar was about a third full, making it easy to find a seat at the bar.

"What are you two drinking?" asked a frail Caucasian woman with big red hair.

Leslie turned to Carson, who wasn't even paying attention.

"I'll take a martini," she said. The bartender gave her a peculiar stare. "Make that two beers and two shots of anything dark."

Leslie swiveled on her stool to face her 'date'.

"So what's going on, Carson?"

"My marriage. It's slipping away from me." The bartender brought two shot glasses and two bottles of Budweiser. Before she could fully put the shot glasses on the wooden bar, Carson took it from her hand and slugged it down.

Leslie held up her glass. "Cheers." She drank.

Leslie looked for the right thing to say. "Maybe she's just . . . going through something. Like a phase."

"Then she should *talk* to me. It's always been us! We don't keep secrets from each other." The lady brought another shot, which Carson drank down.

"So you told your wife about our night together?" Leslie held her shot glass to her lips as she waited for his response.

He grabbed the shot from out of her hands.

"Okay. We have *some* secrets."

"That's what I thought." They laughed.

Carson's laughs faded as he turned to face Leslie seriously.

"I . . . could never admit that to her. That's the only secret I've ever kept from her."

"So go home and tell her. Will that make you feel better?"

Carson's eyes filled with pain as he looked into Leslie's eyes, remembering that night in college when she crept into his dorm room, laid on top of him and made sweet love to him. "You know you really got to me. At one point, I almost left Ebony to see if you and I could have worked together."

Leslie downs the rest of her beer before she speaks.

"It's time to go." She raised her hand and asked for the tab. She slapped her credit card down to pay the bill. Leslie got up without saying a word. Carson followed, confused at her behavior.

Once the car pulled back into the gym parking lot, Leslie sat and waited for Carson to get out.

"What's wrong, Leslie? You haven't spoken to me for the last twenty minutes."

Leslie turned her body to face Carson.

"How *dare* you say that to me now?"

"What? Did I miss something?"

"Do you *know* how long I've been in love with you? How long I've wanted to relive that night in college? How long I've wanted it to be *me* lying next to you, instead of Ebony. And tonight you tell me this shit. Get out!" Her voice became thick as tears caught in her throat. "*GET OUT!*"

Carson obeyed, and stepped out of the car, feeling horrible. He honestly had no idea how she'd felt. Leslie was sexy and playful, so he thought it had just been a game for her, not something serious. He walked around to the driver's side of her car and opened the door. He bent down to her eye-level, and looked into her teary eyes.

"I'm sorry."

Leslie turned to face him. "I'm not *asking* for an apology."

A surge rushed through his body as he grabbed Leslie's face and kissed her so fiercely his lips hurt.

"You're the only one who knows my secrets," he whispered.

Chapter Twenty-Three

Heavy rains fell for the next full week. Ebony and Carson hadn't exchanged anything more than a hi or bye, and neither one knew why. Carson was staying out later than usual, working lots of overtime. It hurt his heart to look at the woman he loved so much, and think how hurt Ebony would be if she found out about Leslie. He didn't think she could never forgive him, if she knew.

Ebony sat around reading a Redbook article on 'How to Spark Up Your Marriage'. The article couldn't keep her attention, so she threw it aside. She turned on the TV, and the movie *Unfaithful* was on, so she quickly turned it off. The rain beat down on the windowpane, and a crash of thunder dimmed the lights. Looking around the empty house, Ebony realized she didn't want to be alone. She grabbed a hooded sweatshirt and ran out to her car. There was only one place she wanted to be so she drove until she pulls up at Jefferson's door without even calling.

The hard rain beat against the metal fire escape that sat behind Jefferson's house. It had been hot and muggy all day; steam rose up from the ground. Ebony peeked through the glass front door. She saw Jefferson standing at his back door, looking out, holding a glass of red wine. She knocked softly on the door, breaking his concentration.

"What are you doing here?" he asked, letting Ebony's soaked form through the door.

Her eyes told him everything as she pushed her way into his place. Without saying a word, she rushed to him and wrapped her hands around the back of his neck, bringing his lips to hers. The two interlocked, dancing across the floor until they run smack into the patio door.

Jefferson looked into her beautiful brown eyes, and she gave him a slight nod, knowing his intentions. He opened the door and dragged Ebony back out into the hard rain. He pushed her wet body onto the stairs, and ripping off her sweatshirt, mussing up her hair, exposing her perky nipples. Within seconds the two were completely naked as the rain showered down on them. Rain drops bounce off Jefferson's as as he climbed between her legs.

She leaned back, letting the rain pelt down on her face. It tickled her body. Ebony pushed him off of her and nudged Jefferson down the stairs. She straddled him and rode his erect length for the next fifteen minutes. He grasped her well-rounded butt and helped keep the steady motion going. Jefferson's inner freak put Ebony face down onto the steps, and slid in from behind, making her scream. He grabbed her hair and rode her like an animal.

"I truly enjoy fucking you." She believed him.

A strange look came over Jefferson's face, and Ebony wondered where his mind had gone.

Chapter Twenty-Four

Mrs. Carmine, a young Hispanic woman that needed to get out of an abusive marriage was Dr. Lovely's first client of the day. It's a hard session to sit through; the woman really needed help. Her sessions were usually two hours long; she always ran over her time. Ebony admired her mom for never charging her for that second hour. As Mrs. Carmine left, she broke down into a hysterical cry after showing Ebony her newest bruises on her thighs and backs.

Mrs. Carmine had only been in the states a few years, and most of her family was still in Mexico. She had three beautiful children under the age of five. Her husband wouldn't let her work, he barely let her leave the house. She was a good mother, but it was hard to care for little ones around the man that broke her down. Her latest bruises were on her back for asking her husband for money to buy milk for the kids, and the one on her stomach because the house wasn't clean to his liking.

Ebony had tears in her eyes. "Mrs. Carmine, personally I don't feel you need a therapist. I think you need the police, a steel bat, and a good support group." Ebony had heard the whole session through the thin walls and said what she thought her mom really wanted to say.

Mrs. Carmine gave a little laugh through her tears. She was afraid to call the police because she doesn't want to get deported. Mrs. Carmine told her husband that she was going to citizenship classes so she can leave the house.

"That's off the record of course." Ebony gave her a hug and the number to a woman's shelter, and opened the office door for her.

"See you next week." Mrs. Carmine returned another hug.

Ebony stared out of the window, thinking what a bad person she was. Mrs. Carmine would have given anything for a husband like Ebony's, and she was taking him for granted. She was lucky she didn't have a husband who beat her. All he wanted to do was love her and provide a good life for her. Her mind also went to the moments she'd shared with Jefferson. He made her body feel things she'd never felt before. The perfect man would have been Carson, mixed with Jefferson's skills in bed. Her thoughts were broken by the door opening.

She jumped up out of her seat in surprise. "What are you doing here?"

"After last night, I needed to see you." Jefferson closed the door behind him.

"It was a mistake. Our *last* one. You need to leave. I am *erasing* you from my life." Ebony walked towards the door and opened it for him to leave. She was embarrassed by how she'd acted last night, but part of her still didn't regret it.

"You don't really mean that, or you wouldn't have shown up at my place last night." He stepped closer, making her nervous. "The way you fucked me last night? It shows you're not done with me."

"Sshhh! My mother will hear you."

Jefferson slowly ran his hands from the side of her ear down to her chin, circling his hand around the back of her neck and pulling her lips into his. The passionate kiss made her knees wobble. Ebony returned the kiss, drunk on the feeling of being so wanted by a man. She was so taken by her kiss, she didn't notice her husband standing in the doorway.

Chapter Twenty-Five

Carson ran from the building, distraught. His tears clouded his vision, causing him to run right into a crowded street. He barely missed the oncoming traffic. Ebony's betrayal was more than he can stand. Carson knew his marriage hadn't been right for some time, and he knew deep down that part of it was his fault. Jefferson's presence was all his fault.

The left side of his brain was telling him to go back upstairs and kick Jefferson's ass and end the whole mess, but he knew he wasn't that man. Carson had always been a docile man. He believed Ebony loved him for that. She wasn't the type of woman that needed a strong, dominating man, but part of him wished he was like that. Instead of defending his honor and the honor of his wife, he decided to go to his favorite place to blow off steam: the gym.

<hr/>

"Back again, Mr. Brody?" The young woman behind the counter greeted him for the second time that day. He gave her a half-smile trying, to be polite but not wanting to talk, either. After stopping in the locker room, he headed straight for a treadmill and started running as fast as he could. With sweat pouring down his face, Carson slid right off the treadmill, losing his composure.

"If you're not careful, you'll pass out."

He looked up through exhausted eyes at Leslie.

"How are you?" she asked.

His green eyes looked on her blankly. He couldn't think of anything coherent to say. He was still embarrassed by their last encounter, and was hoping to avoid her for a while.

"I should apologize for the other night."

"No, I should for the way I behaved. I just let old feelings cloud my mind." Carson looked at her and could tell that her feelings for him were still very real. All the actions of the last few days played in his head, and the tears started flowing from his eyes.

"What do you see in me? I'm a weak, pathetic man."

"What is *wrong* with you?" she asked.

Carson straightened himself up quickly. "Nothing, I just need to be alone."

He turned to walk away when Leslie reached for his arm.

"Let me come with you?"

She saw he was in no condition to be alone . . . and she wanted his company. He grabbed his bag and met Leslie by the front door. The odd couple jumped into Leslie's 2-door black convertible BMW. She drove fifteen minutes down the interstate to a quaint condo. Like a lost puppy, Carson followed her into her home.

"What's your poison? Beer, wine, or something a little stronger?" Leslie's voice trailed off as she went into the kitchen.

"Stronger, please."

He followed the sound of her high heels against the linoleum floor, and found Leslie's ass bent over in the refrigerator. He came up behind her, reaching on top of her refrigerator, grabbing a bottle of Patron. He poured himself a shot and quickly gulped it down and refilled it. Leslie stood up watching Carson drown his sorrows. The coldness of the icebox made her nipples protrude through her shirt. Thoughts of Ebony and Jefferson filled his mind, and the visual of the two blurred his vision.

He stepped to Leslie and couldn't resist grabbing her breasts thinking of revenge. She let out a moan as his hand ran up under her skirt, along her thigh. Having an out-of-body experience, he reached for her panties and ripped them off her. It hurt a little. She didn't mind. He spun her forward and slammed her back into the fridge. The buttons on her silk blouse flew all over the kitchen as Carson took a rougher approach.

"You want me? How badly do you want this dick?" Carson spoke in a nastier tone he'd never used before.

Leslie was taken aback by his words. She'd never seen the rough side of Carson before. He pulled down his pants, revealing his erect member. He shoved it into Leslie while they stood. He was inflicting more pain than pleasure.

"Is this what you want, bitch? Answer me! You want to be treated like the ho you are??"

Leslie pushed Carson off of her.

"Stop it!"

Her screams brought him back to reality. Carson let go of her and fell to the cold floor, realizing what he'd done. Tears ran from his eyes as he lost control of his emotions.

Leslie leaned against the fridge, catching her breath. "You asked me earlier what I saw in you?"

Carson couldn't bring himself to meet her eyes.

"You're a man who wears his heart on his sleeve. You care *so deeply* for the people around you that you need to make everyone around you happy. It's your best asset. You're not a fighter. You're a lover and a damn good friend."

Leslie slumped to the floor with Carson and embraced him like a child. The two sat there in silence for half an hour. It reminded her of college, when they used to sit under a tree for hours and just enjoy the silence. It always calmed Carson.

In the next room, Carson's cell phone broke the silence. Carson dragged his body off the floor.

"Can I use your bathroom?"

Carson turned both knobs on the sink until it was running warm. He splashed the water over his face, trying to wash away the memory of the last few hours. His soggy face stared at him in the mirror, trying to answer the question, *what went wrong?* Ebony was the one woman he felt would never betray him. Not like this. Carson wasn't a violent man, but at that very moment, he wanted to *pound* on Jefferson. His fist came down on the bathroom counter with a *thunk*.

A knock came. "You okay in there?"

"I'll be right out." Carson took one last look at himself, and joined Leslie in her living room. She handed him a cold beer. "You want to talk about it now?"

He stared at the bottle in his hands. "I haven't had one of these since college." The cool bottle touched his lips as he leaned his head back, enjoying the smoothness going down his throat. In a matter of seconds, the bottle was empty.

"My marriage is over . . ." It came out as a whisper. "I caught Ebony in the arms of another man, and I don't know how to survive without her."

He laid his head against Leslie's comforting chest. She gave his forehead a kiss, a devilish smile appears across her face, as she told him he'd be all right.

Chapter Twenty-Six

As the sun chased the moon away, Carson woke up in the arms of a woman other than his wife. A woman who'd loved him and longed for him since high school. Leslie was never the prettiest or most popular girl. That had been Ebony. She loathed Ebony and it wasn't 'til her breasts grew in, her glasses disappeared, and her baby fat took shape that Leslie became noticed. It was no accident she ended up at the same college as Carson. Her plan to land him was born the moment she'd laid eyes on him. Sophomore year of college was when it all started to happen.

There was a huge fraternity party at the Kappa house. Since finals had just wrapped up, everyone was there. Carson was hanging with his boy Mike when Leslie entered the party, alone. They saw each other across the crowded room. She strolled right up to him and asked him to dance to a Mary J. Blige song.

"How 'bout you get me a drink?" She asked once the song switched over.

"I guess I can manage, since they're free." They shared a laugh and a few more drinks, until they found themselves outside talking by the pool.

"So, how serious are you and Ebony?" She asked bluntly.

Carson blinked. "We've been together forever."

She leaned in a little closer. "That's not what I asked you."

Carson pulled away; the smell of alcohol on her breath was too much for him. "I love her. She's my world and I plan on marrying her once we graduate." She crept back into his personal space. "So she's the *only* woman you're ever going to sleep with?"

His adam's apple took a jump as he swallowed hard. "I, ah, don't know what you mean."

"You don't have to be afraid." Leslie scooted closer and started unbuttoning his pants. Carson reached for her wrist to stop the motion, but she'd already managed to pull his dick out and wrap her drunken lips around it.

"Ohhhh my gosh." One thing led to another and the two of them got it on right in the bushes. Once they returned to the party, Ebony met Carson with a million questions, wondering where he'd been. Leslie smiled as she walked past Ebony . . . and the night was never brought up again.

Chapter Twenty-Seven

The house was quiet as Carson arrived to take a shower and get some real sleep. Ebony wasn't home and he was thankful for that. How could he possibly look her in the face after being with Leslie last night? Even though he knew deep down that the kiss he saw his wife share with Jefferson must have been deeper than that. He'd be a fool to think otherwise. Carson started cleaning up the house that was starting to resemble a bachelor pad. On the coffee table, he noticed their wedding album open, so he reviewed the happiest day of his life until the front door opens.

"What are you doing?" asked Ebony, as she slowly entered the room.

"Just reminiscing." Carson patted an empty spot on the couch, motioning for her to join him. They continued to silently flip through the album pages, through to the very last page where they were sharing their first kiss as man and wife. Carson looked at Ebony.

His voice was quiet and calm. "Jefferson . . . do you want him?"

She looked at him, confused.

"I saw you two the other day at the office."

Ebony hung her head in shame. No words could ease his hurt. His face showing all the pain that his body was feeling.

Their eyes meet and question marks run over their pupils.

"And last night, where were you, Carson?"

". . . Honestly?"

Ebony gave him a stern look; she wasn't in the mood for bullshit.

"I spent the night at Leslie's, but nothing happened. I had a few drinks and passed out on her couch."

Ebony stood up, indignant. Carson shot that down immediately.

"*Hell* no. You don't *do* that. I saw you kiss Jefferson at your office, so don't look at me like *I'm* the one cheating."

Her head whipped around in fury to face her husband.

"Yes! I made a mistake! But my ass was at home last night, not with another woman!"

Nothing more was said, that night. Ebony couldn't even look at her husband . . . or herself, in the mirror. She knew she'd betrayed her husband worse than he had her, and deep down she knew Carson didn't sleep with Leslie. Now he knew about Jefferson. Ebony wanted to walk away, but Jefferson had a sexiness to him that was so addictive and frightening at the same time.

Chapter Twenty-Eight

*M*ichael was throwing a party at a swanky club in the city. Ebony promised Carson she'd meet him there after work, despite the tension between them. Ebony got to work feeling refreshed, since she didn't have to share her bed last night.

The last client of the day was Samantha Gray, who actually put her in a good mood with her funny antics about men. As Ebony began to wrap up her day, the office door creaked. She turned around to see Jefferson standing in her doorway.

"I can't do this. Not today. I have to be somewhere."

Jefferson nodded. "So do I. I just stopped by for a minute."

Jefferson strode to her with confidence. Ebony backed up, hitting the wall behind her desk. His firm hand reached for her blouse and she swatted it away.

"Don't be like that. We've only a few minutes."

"Ebony, I—" Her mother stepped out of her office, noticing her daughter in a compromising position. Ebony ducked away from Jefferson.

"Yes, mom?" Ebony blushed.

"I'm leaving for the day. Are you ready to go?" Her mother gave Jefferson an evil look.

"I'll be right behind you, mom. I'm just gonna lock up."

"Okay, but hurry. I'm sure your *husband* is waiting for you."

Jefferson smirked at Ebony's mother. She left the office hesitantly. Jefferson turned to Ebony, grabbing her arm and pulling her into her mother's office.

She no longer put up a fight as he unbuttoned her blouse and let the gentle material float to the floor. She covered herself with her hands.

"I don't know why you're acting this way."

"*What* way?" she questioned.

"Your shy act doesn't work. It's cute in public, but we're alone now."

Ebony ducked to her left and freed herself from his grasp.

"My mother'll come back." She started to put back on her same blouse. "And my husband *is* waiting for me".

"And?" he paused, not caring. "I'm right *here* for you." He pointed down to the bulge in his pants.

Jefferson took one step forward; Ebony took one back. He took another step and she moved another step back. Deep down, she hungered for this man, but he also left her with a *nervous* feeling she couldn't shake. Ebony's steps ended when she backed right into the chaise lounge where patients usually lay.

"Baby, you can't get away from me." He came so close to her, she could feel his breath on the tip of her nose. His head tilted down like he was going to kiss her until he grabbed her inch waist and spun her around. Yet again, her blouse hits the floor. Jackson put the tips of his fingers at the top of her back, and slowly moved his hand down her spine with light pressure. Ebony pressed her back into his hands, liking his firm touch. He stoppe at her waistline and unzipped her brown skirt. Once undone, the skirt joined the blouse, and Ebony was left in a matching Calvin Klein beige panty set and a pair of brown heels. Jackson took a tiny step back to admire his view. There was something about a half-naked woman in heels that drove him crazy.

"Turn around." She did as she was told.

"Take those panties off." She did as she was told.

Usually, Ebony didn't like to be dominated, but when Jefferson told her to do something, she felt compelled to obey. She bent down at the waist and rolled her lace panties all the way to her ankles, stepping out of them. She eyed Jefferson, trying to read his thoughts. She was hoping he'd pleasure her the same way he did before. Since her eyes had been opened to new things, she'd become obsessed.

Jefferson positioned her on the chaise lounge, and parted her legs just wide enough for him to slip in between. He dove in face-first, tasting Ebony again like it was her first time. Her face scrunched up as she tried to contain her feelings. She didn't want to scream. Not at work.

When Jackson felt Ebony had truly enjoyed herself, he stood up and pulled her up. He bent her brown-skinned body over the back of the chaise and entered her from behind. She let out a slight moan from his first insertion. Jefferson got a steady rhythm going, grabbing her hair and pulling back on it like he was riding a horse. His pace grew faster and faster, until he smacked her bare ass with his free hand, gave her one last hard push. He let out a loud moan.

The two stood there, trying to catch their breath. Ebony caught a glimpse of the clock and noticed it was 9:30PM.

"Oh my gosh." She dashed over to her mom's closet and grabbed a fresh blouse. She was thankful the two of them were the same size, and ran off to the bathroom to clean herself up and get ready for the party. Jefferson opened a window to let the room air out.

She was furious with Jackson for coming there and making her late. She also had to scrub the smell of sex off her in a public bathroom, and think of a lie for her husband as to why she was so late.

Twenty minutes later, she came out of the bathroom, looking and smelling brand new. The office was now empty, so she turned off the lights and rushed out into the night.

Ebony was a little perturbed by the fact that she'd just had a 'booty call' without even a kiss or a goodbye. Now, at five minutes to ten, she hopped in her car and made her way to Club Indigo.

The club was packed like she knew it would be, but Carson's was still the first face she saw. His eyes grew with excitement as he greeted her with a kiss.

Ebony was still busy concocting a lie, when Carson stopped her.

"Your mom called and told me you got stuck at the office. Everything okay?"

Ebony was puzzled. Why would her mom lie for her?

"It's fine. Just paperwork."

"Well, I'm glad you're here." He kissed her again, this time on the cheek. Knowing her husband, Ebony felt this was his way of putting all the stuff from last night behind him without really dealing with the issues.

"Want a drink?"

"Can you get me a Cosmo?"

Carson nodded his head and made his way to the bar. Surveying the club, looking for familiar faces, Ebony spotted a face she'd just seen half an hour earlier.

She moved full speed ahead to the other side of the room, where Jefferson was laughing it up with some girl in a tight mini-skirt.

"Excuse us," said Ebony. She pulled Jefferson out from the woman's grip. She smacked his arm, and whispered sharply in his ear. "Don't *do* that again! You made me feel like your whore. That's not me."

He laughed at her anger. "I know. 'Cause if you were one of my whores I wouldn't eat your p—"

"*Don't* say that word." He laughed even louder. Jefferson leaned into her ear. "You *know* you're much more than that." He licked the inside of her ear. She giggled like a school girl.

Carson walks back to the spot he'd left Ebony, carrying her drink. He looked around, hoping Ebony just went to the bathroom. A sea of people seemed to part, and he caught a glimpse of his wife.

Furious, Carson saw Jackson's right arm around her waist like she was about to float away. The look on her face was one of great joy, and Carson realized Ebony smiled from his conversation. It was a look of lust, passion, and pure contentment. Jefferson's lips came close to her ear again. She blushed, then backed away, sensing something was wrong.

Feeling a pair of eyes on her, she looked in Carson's direction and felt his anger from twenty feet away. Her smile quickly faded. She left Jefferson and returned to her rightful place by her husband, all the while, eyeing her lover from across the room. She took a sip of her drink and felt a burning desire to be back in his arms. She yearned for the day she could show up to a party with the finest man she'd ever laid eyes on around her arm, to display him for every woman in the place. Carson grabbed her arm and started to squeeze.

"You're hurting me!" Carson released slightly.

"Baby, I'm sorry. That man just makes me so *mad*."

A small vein starts rose on his forehead. "I thought he was your boy?"

"Not really." Carson grabbed his wife's drink from her hand and drank the whole thing in one gulp.

"Let's go!"

Ebony stared at the empty glass, put it on the bar, and ran after her husband, turned on.

Chapter Twenty-Nine

"We need to talk. Meet me at my office in half an hour." Carson slammed the phone down and rushed out the house before his wife could question him. Before long, he and Michael stood over Carson's desk at his office.

Michael pulled up a chair. "What's the big emergency? I haven't even had my morning drink."

"We have coffee."

"I'm not talking about coffee." Michael produced a flask from his jacket pocket and took a pull. "Okay. Talk."

"Man, I'm going crazy." Carson paced back and forth. "Jefferson is *everywhere,* he's moving in on my wife, and I can't do anything about it. She's a sucker for aggressive men, so I know she's falling for him. I just need to get her *away* from all this."

"Dude, you're making me dizzy. Sit your ass down!" Michael took out his flask again and put it in front of Carson. "Take a pull."

Carson took a long drink and put the flask back down.

". . . Better?"

Carson shook his head in agreement.

"Now, if you want to get your wife away from him, then take her on vacation or something. But honestly, *nothing'll* be fixed until you two clear the air and get the truth out. I know how you and Leslie were in college, and you can't go changing the past, well . . ."

Carson laid his head down on his desk, defeated. He knew how stupid he sounded, not fighting for his marriage, but he wasn't a fighter! Still. The only person in the world he *would* fight for, was his wife. "You're right, I'll tell her. I confessed I fell asleep at Leslie's the other night, and she took it pretty well."

"Ebony . . . can be reasonable." Michael didn't really believe what he was saying, but friends didn't always resort to complete honesty.

"And if she leaves me, then that's what it's gonna be. But she wouldn't leave me for that sorry-ass man!" Carson stood, getting his confidence back.

He and Michael shared a hug. Michael left his flask on the desk. "You might need it."

⌘

Ebony strolled into her office. Little did she know her life would soon change forever.

"Morning, Jessica."

Jessica, the receptionist for Dr. Richards, gave her a sullen nod. "Good morning, Mrs. Brody."

Ebony realized she hadn't heard that name in a while. Being called Mrs. Brody made her feel a sense of pride. She'd always wanted that name . . . but at the same time, she wasn't fit to carry it just now.

"I left a newspaper on your desk. I just wanted to say I'm sorry." Ebony gave her a strange look. What could she possible feel sorry about?

"Would you like some coffee this morning?"

"No thanks." Ebony looks at her strangely. *We have the same job,* she thought, *why would she get me coffee?* As she settled into her chair, her eyes looked down at the *New York Post*. The headline read, *Man Kills Wife and Kids*. Ebony fell back as she read the article and saw the name of the first victim, Mrs. Carmine! According to the paper, her husband finally snapped. He beat them, put them in their car and ran it into the river.

"Oh my god! . . . I think I'll take that coffee now."

Melody scurried into the office to find Ebony, face down on her desk.

"Ebony?" she whispered, "Are you okay sweetie?" Ebony shook her head without lifting it up. Melody put her hand on her shoulder. She heard Ebony sobbing.

"Let's get out of here." Melody took her hand, and went to Jessica. "Can you cover for Ebony for a while?" She nodded in agreement. "And please don't show Dr. Lovely the newspaper until after she's done with her last client of the day. Okay?"

Jessica nodded again. "Of course."

The two friends walk down the street to a small coffee shop on the corner. Melody ordered two strawberry smoothies.

"I'm your therapist today. Talk to me, sweetie."

Ebony looked up with watery eyes and took a long sip of her smoothie.

"I gave her some advice that my mother would be *pissed* if she ever found out about it. I *knew* what he'd done to her, and what did I do? Nothing. I gave her a *card* and that's all. Her death is on my hands." Ebony broke out in uncontrollable sobs. Melody looked around as other customers started to stare. She took Ebony's hand.

"I know this may sound harsh . . . but it's not your fault. You *didn't* put her in an abusive relationship and it wasn't for you to get her out of it. You told her what she needed to do, and you gave her a way out. What else could you do? If it had been me, you'd have dragged me out of that house butt naked and all, but you couldn't do that for her. You paved the way for her, there's not much more you could have done. *I* feel bad for your mother."

Melody handed her sobbing friend some tissues.

"Life is just so short," Ebony managed. She dried her eyes. "You just never know when it's going to be over . . . and what'll I have to show for it?"

Melody grew concerned. "What are you saying, Ebony? Is there something you want out of life that you're not getting?"

Ebony reached into her purse and pulled out the card from the record producer.

". . . Jefferson took me to this club and I got to *sing*. I felt so alive, and I realized how much I missed it."

"Then go for it!"

Ebony stood and hugged her best friend.

Ebony picked up her phone and called the producer to set up an appointment for Friday night. She and Melody spent the rest of the day shopping in the city, to find the perfect outfit for her meeting.

"Don't forget: we also have to get to Carson's championship game tonight."

Melody smiled weakly. "Sweaty men in shorts, I wouldn't miss it."

Chapter Thirty

*I*t was Wednesday night, and the girls were running late for the last game of the season. Dressed to impress, the girls entered the gym in fitted tees, baby phat jeans, and three-inch heels. Two guys towering over six feet were jumping for the ball. Ebony waved to Carson like everything was good between them. She never missed a game and wasn't going to start now.

As the two friends took a seat on the bleachers, Melody noticed Jefferson on the other team and nudged Ebony's shoulder.

"Are you *kidding me*? Everywhere I turn, there he is!"

"You've got to cut *all* ties from him, and work on getting your marriage back."

Ebony nodded. "I know, I know".

Sitting on the bench, Carson looked up at his wife and blew her a kiss. Ebony smiled, feeling like when they had just started dating. So many years ago, she knew she was the only one for him, and he always made her feel like the most important person in the room.

After he blew her a kiss, she noticed him waving at someone sitting on the opposite side of the gym. Ebony looked up at her nemesis, Leslie.

"What the hell is *she* doing here?" Ebony asked Melody, livid.

"How should I know?"

"Carson's waving at her. I know he didn't invite her."

"Why do you hate her so much?"

"All through college, she tried to take him from me, and I didn't play that. You don't mess with my man!"

"Look, 'your man' is going in." Melody nudged Ebony and they let out a cheer, until they realized Carson was guarding *Jefferson* who had a few inches and about twenty pounds of muscle on him.

"That's *not* good," said Ebony.

The game which was intensely physical, and a very close match. They only played two fifteen-minute halves since it wasn't the NBA, which was long enough for men over thirty. With four minutes left and Carson's team down by five, Carson couldn't lose to his arch enemy, so he kicked it up a notch. Jefferson had the ball, running down the court with Carson on his heels. Jefferson went up for the lay-up and Carson went up with him, blocking the ball and coming down on him with his elbow.

"Foul!" shouted the referee. Jefferson smiled menacingly at Carson. They headed back down the court, with Carson dribbling the ball. Carson stopped to shoot the ball from the foul line when Jefferson ran right into his back, pushing him to the ground. Carson landed right on his nose. He jumped up with blood dripping down his lip, and punched Jefferson in the jaw.

Jefferson took the punch, and lunged back at Carson. They rolled on the ground, blood going everywhere. Ebony jumped to her feet, yelling for someone to stop the fight. The referee blew the whistle for them to stop, but no-one intervened. Michael jumped in and pulled his boy out of the brawl.

"Calm down, dude," he coached his friend.

"Yeah . . . calm down." Jefferson said with a laugh.

"*This isn't over.*" Carson spat out blood as he made his way back to the locker room.

"I told you it wasn't good."

Melody looked at her best friend, thinking the fight wouldn't have happened if not for her betrayal, but she wisely kept the thought to herself.

⁓❧⁓

Ebony rushed into the house, to find Carson sitting at their kitchen table with a plastic bag of ice on his nose. She went to him, took the ice from him, and held it in place for him.

"That was some show. I've never seen you play like that."

Carson looked up at her, ashamed of how he'd acted. He'd never been in a fight, and his face was proof of that. Ebony could see how hurt Carson was. "Actually?" she said, forcing a smile. "It was kinda sexy!"

Carson looked her in the eyes, and the two of them started laughing.

Chapter Thirty-One

The next morning, Ebony woke up before her husband. She rolled over and stared at his swollen nose, and wondered how their life came to be so crazy. She had decisions to make, and needed to change her life before it went completely out of control.

Carson stirred and opened his eyes.

"Morning, handsome."

"Hey, what time is it?" he asked, groggily.

"After ten." Carson jumped up in alarm. "Relax, baby. I already called your office."

He laid back down. "Thanks."

". . . So, you ready to talk about it?" She quietly asked.

"There's not much to say. I'm embarrassed about how I acted. Maybe I should make an appointment with your mom."

Ebony smiled, remembering why she loved him so much. Carson put his head down and lets out a deep breath. Ebony's smile faded, for fear of what he was going to say next. He pulls his head up slowly. "Have you and Jefferson . . . been inappropriate with each other?"

Ebony turned her back to Carson.

"*What?!* What would make you say something like that??"

He sat up, angry. "Don't you talk to me like I'm stupid. I *saw* the two of you at my birthday party. Really, Ebony, in *our house?* What was that?"

Ebony turned back towards Carson in disbelief. She'd never heard him talk like that before. She knew this was her doorway to the truth, if she could actually cross through.

"I didn't invite him to your party, or the wedding, or basketball, or anything else. You brought him into our lives, not me."

"That wasn't my question, but you just answered it, thanks."

Carson got out of the bed, walked to the bathroom and shut the door. Tears ran down Ebony's face as her fears came to light. She'd wanted her affair to end before Carson found out. But even though she'd kept it a secret, he knew anyway. She knew how much she'd hurt him, and he didn't deserve any of it.

Ebony grabbed a suitcase out of the basement and started packing a few days' worth of clothes when the bathroom door opened.

"What are you doing?"

"I'm going to spend a few days with India and take care of some business. I'm sorry for hurting you . . . if that means anything." Ebony zipped the bag shut. She grabbed her purse and was out the door.

"It's partly my fault, too," said Carson, stopping her in her tracks.

"What is?"

"Jefferson." He took his wife's hand from the bag and led her to the bed. "You know the saying, keep your friends close, but your enemies closer?" She nodded. "Jefferson knows a secret about me and I didn't want it to come out . . . but it doesn't matter anymore."

Ebony's curiosity was peaked. "Go on."

"Back in college, Jefferson and I were roommates for a few months, before he left school. He knows about something that happened . . ."

"Carson, please just spit it out." Ebony was losing patience.

"Leslie and I slept together." Her mouth dropped open. "It was at a party and . . ."

"Stop! Please. I don't want to hear anymore." She took her hand from his. "I have to go catch my train. See you in a few days."

She walked to the door and stopped. She looked back at her husband, who was sprawled out on the bed on the edge of tears.

"I guess we're even, then, because I slept with Jefferson."

She turned back around and walked out the room. Carson's fears were confirmed. The tears poured from his face. Carson didn't know if his wife was leaving for the weekend, or leaving their marriage for good.

Chapter Thirty-Two

The train pulled into the station a little after 3PM, Friday afternoon. Her sister lived about six blocks from the station, so she did what any true New Yorker did: walk. She forgot how much she hated the crowds of the city, but loved to visit. As she walked past Broadway, she decided she'd liked to see a matinee show on Saturday; something she hasn't done in years.

Ebony walked up to her sister's studio apartment.

"Hey sis, I'm here." She and India hugged.

"So what's going on?" India took her sister's bag and welcomed her in.

"Carson and I aren't doing well."

"Is this about that guy you cheated with?"

Ebony walked into the kitchen to get a drink. She needed something strong, if this type of talk was going to happen so early in the day.

"He cheated on me in college with that woman I hate, and *I* cheated with someone I thought was his friend. The truth is finally out."

Ebony threw her hands up in the air and took a long deep breath.

"So now what?" India flopped down on her futon next to her sister.

"I don't know. I guess if we love each other, then we should repair our marriage . . . but Jefferson makes me feel things I've never felt, and opened my eyes to things. I get excited when I'm with him."

"So your marriage is over?"

"What are you a reporter? Why the 20 questions?" She took a long drink. "I don't have any answers yet, I'm just glad to be away and clear my head."

Later that evening, Ebony arrived at the address the producer had given her. From the outside, it looks like an apartment building. But once inside, it was a huge three-story studio. The main floor seemed to be empty.

"Hello! Mr. Weber?"

A figure appeared from behind a curtain. As he came into the light, she recognized him from the club.

"So glad you called me." He extended his hand to her. "Call me Leo."

"Ebony." The two shook hands. Leo turned and walked off, and Ebony followed.

"I haven't stopped thinking about your voice," said Leo. "I had my people work up some songs that I think would be great for your voice."

Ebony stopped walking. "You—you want me to record a song?"

Leo turned around and smiled. "Little lady, I want you to record an *album*."

Ebony smiled, feeling happier and more fulfilled than she had in ages.

"Is that not what you want?" asked Leo.

"I've really only sung for fun; never professionally."

"Well, let's record one song and see what you think. If you're horrible, then you just wasted a few hours of my time, and I'll charge you $100 for the studio time."

Ebony's smile disappeared, and concern filled her face. She wondered if this was a good idea after all.

". . . but if you're great, you'll make me a lot of money . . . and some for you too." She laughed uneasily, not knowing how to take this guy, or what to think of him. A heavy-set man appeared from the back room.

"This is Joe, he's going to lay down the track with you." Ebony shook his hand. "Shall we begin?" She nodded, and followed them back to a small recording booth.

Leo handed her the music, and Joe played. After about thirty minutes of studying the words, Joe pressed 'record' and her voice was laid on the track. Two hours later, and several takes, the song was finally done. When the song was played back, Ebony's eyes fill with joy. She couldn't believe the sound coming out of the speaker.

"That isn't me! Is it?"

"You're the only lady in here," Joe said with a smile.

Leo came over with a contract. "As you can see, we're just a small recording company right now, but I *do* have the resources to make this happen . . . if you let me."

"Okay. Let me read over this contract, and I'll fax it back to you in the morning." Leo smiled, realizing she was no fool.

He nodded in agreement. "Sure, just don't wait too long, because I can't do anything until I have your signature."

"I will."

Ebony grabbed her things to leave.

"Oh, don't forget this." Joe handed her a copy of the CD. "Hope to see you soon."

She took the CD and walked out. She texted her sister, to meet her and celebrate. It was a little after midnight, but since the clubs in the meat packing district didn't close until 4AM, so Ebony was ready to party.

Ebony took a cab ride to a dimly lit club with a hot pink canopy. The music was blaring out the front door as the bouncer opened it every few minutes, only letting a few people in at a time.

Ebony took her place in line, hoping her sister would get there before she reached the front. A group of three young girls in front of her looked behind them and start laughing. Ebony looks behind her to see what was so funny, until she realized they were laughing at *her*. She had no idea why.

She looked herself over, thinking her outfit was cute. She studied the girls, noticing each was showing their stomach, breasts, or butt hanging out of their outfit. She laughed thinking those girls remind her of herself just a few years ago, but she'd always gotten more respect being fully clothed. India finally pulled up in a cab as the three girls were let into the club.

"What's going on, sis?"

"Do I look okay?" India looked her sister up and down, and shrugged.

"You could touch up your lips, but yeah. Why?"

"These three girls were laughing at me."

India shrugged. "This is a young people's club. Don't worry about them. You were like them, at their age."

"Not quite." Ebony laughed as the bouncer motions for them to step forward. Once in the club, Ebony heads straight to the bar.

"First round's on me."

"If we do it right, we won't have to pay for any drinks," India smiles.

The two grabbed a pair of cranberry and vodkas, and move to the dance floor. Ebony felt on top of the world. She danced with young men, laughing, and enjoying the time with her sister.

"We really need to do this more often. I miss you!" Ebony was getting mushy, which meant she was feeling her drink. India gave her sister a hug, and a few men looked over, hoping they'd get a show.

"I need a refill." Ebony held up her empty glass, and made her way back to the bar. She ordered another drink. As she dug in her purse for some cash, but the bartender told her the drink was already paid for. She pointed to a sexy, clean-cut young man standing with the same three girls from outside of the club. Ebony looked in his direction. He excused himself from the girls and made his way to Ebony.

"I've been watching you all evening, and you are *stunning.*"

"Well! Thank you for the drink, and for the compliment."

Ebony looked past the man at the girls. She held up her drink and winked at the angry trio.

"Thanks again for the drink." Ebony turned to walk away from the bar.

"That's all I get? Can I at lease have a dance, or maybe your name?"

"Ebony." She extended her hand to shake his.

"One dance?"

They moved to the dance floor, and Ebony spent the next thirty minutes dancing with him. She was pleasantly surprised how much she enjoyed his company. She felt a little guilty to leave Carson sitting at home . . . but only a little.

Chapter Thirty-Three

That Saturday, Carson was stretched out on a recliner in his basement, flipping through channels on TV. He looked over at his cell phone, sitting on an end table. He picked it up, missing his wife. But since she hasn't bothered to call *him*, he decided to leave it alone. Carson thought back about five years, when he and Ebony used to spend the weekends going to farmers' markets or vineyards, or museums, anything to fill their days and spend time together. Why had his life turned upside down? Why had Jefferson come back after all those years? What did he have to gain? And *why* was he going after Ebony?

His thoughts were broken by a knock at the front door. He ran up the steps, hoping it was his wife, knowing it probably wasn't the case. He opened the door.

"Why haven't you answered your phone?" asked Michael, not even bothering with a hello.

"Hi to you, too."

Michael made his way into the house, leaving Carson there holding the door open.

"Shut the door man, you're letting bugs in."

"I really want to be alone, Mike."

"Too bad."

Carson rolled his eyes.

"How long have I known you, Carson?"

"I don't know, twenty years."

"And have I ever steered you wrong?"

Carson looked at Michael in disbelief. For every bit of trouble he'd ever gotten into, Michael had been there. When he got him to skip school when they were teenagers, or borrow his father's sports car to go to a party, or when Michael convinced Carson that the head cheerleader in high school wanted him. Instead; it led to Carson getting his butt kicked.

"Yeah, I can think of a few times."

"Forget all that. I can't let you just sit here while your wife is off living it up. So get your butt up, put some clothes on, and stop moping. Your world doesn't revolve around Ebony—though I love her to death—but come on man, you look pathetic."

He wanted to tell Michael that his wife had cheated on him, but he couldn't bring himself to say the words out loud. He wanted to *get even* with Jefferson; not go out and party. He wanted to talk things out with his wife and have her come home.

Carson looked at himself in the mirror in the hallway and smiled. He was a nice-looking man, and shouldn't have sat at home, wondering what his wife was doing.

"You're right. I'll go get dressed."

He ran upstairs and got in the shower. Twenty minutes later, a new Carson stepped out. They decided to go to Dave and Buster's to have some drinks and play some games. By nightfall, Michael had Carson drinking beer, and the two of them decided to go to T.G. I. Friday's to get something to eat. They grabbed two seats at the bar.

The bartender brought them menus. "Well gents, it's ladies' night so you can enjoy the scenery, but the discounts on drinks go to girls. Sorry."

"I'm good with that," said Michael. We've got money and you have sexy ladies . . . including yourself. Can we start with an order of wings and a couple of beers?"

Carson shook his head. "You know I don't like beer. It never ends well."

Michael waved him off as he surveyed the scenery. There was a DJ set up in the corner of the bar, playing old school rap, Carson's favorite. The sexy bartender came back with two tall dark beers, and two shot glasses.

Carson shook his head. "We didn't order these."

"I know. She did."

She pointed across the bar at Leslie, sitting with a date. Leslie raised her own shot glass and waited for Carson and Michael to do the same. The three of them took the shots together, and Carson mouthed the words 'thank you' across the bar. He really didn't want the shot, but he didn't want to look like a punk in front of Leslie.

"It seems like she and Jefferson are everywhere nowadays." Carson said, as his liquor went straight to his head. "Excuse me."

Carson got up to use the bathroom. Beer always ran right through him. As he washed his hands, the bathroom door opened and he heard heels on the tiles. Carson quickly turned and saw Leslie standing in front of the door.

"What are you doing?" he asked.

"I should ask *you* that. Why aren't you home with your wife?"

". . . She left me."

Leslie opened her mouth in a state of shock.

"That ungrateful bitch!"

"She went to the city for the weekend."

Leslie slowly walks towards him.

"So you're alone for the weekend?"

"Not exactly. Michael was trying to cheer me up, as you can see."

Carson headed to the door, and Leslie blocked it.

"I mean later. You need some company?"

She reached out, grabbing his shirt and pulling him to her. Carson knew he was a little drunk. Leslie brings her glossy lips right up to his.

"Female company. We never did finish the other night."

She grabbed Carson's hand and put it between her legs, moving it up and down, rubbing him against on her. She brought his hand up to her mouth and licked his fingers one by one. Carson lost his balance and stumbled against the door. Leslie smiled as she looks down at his erection, protruding through his pants.

"I gotta go."

He pushed Leslie to the side and ran out of the bathroom. He returned to the bar.

"What, did you fall in? You've been gone a while."

"No! Leslie damn near jumped me in the bathroom."

"And you're complaining because . . . ?"

"I'm *married*." Carson picked up his glass and took a long sip. He saw Leslie walk back over to her date and winked at Carson.

"She wants you bad!" Michael's laughing was uncontrollable. "Just fuck her and give her what she wants."

"I did that once, and I can't do that again."

Carson didn't bother bringing up the incident at Leslie's house.

"Can we order? I'm starving." Carson waved the bartender over. He ordered a Jack Daniels steak, and Michael asked for pasta. After a few more beers, Carson went over and thanked Leslie again for the drinks. He and Michael left. It was 9PM, and Carson was ready to wind down.

"We're not going home yet. It wouldn't *kill* you to stay out a little past your bedtime. It's not like you're going home to anyone."

Carson took out his cell phone and texted his wife to say he was thinking of her, and missed her. Michael continued his 'kidnapping' spree and took Carson to a club he'd never seen before.

"I don't think I can dance, man. I'm wasted."

"That's good, Carson, 'cause this isn't that type of club."

Carson looked up at the neon sign that read *Gentleman's Club*.

"Oh no!"

Michael started laughing and grabbed his boy's arm. "You can't be a man and never have been to a strip club. This was how we *should* have spent your last night as a free man. Better late than never."

Carson thought back to his bachelor party when he and his boys went to a pool hall. He'd really enjoyed himself that night. Carson looked at Michael, wondering how they'd been friends so long with such different tastes and interests.

They walked into the club. "Ten dollar cover," said the bouncer. Michael looked to Carson. "You got me bro? I don't have any cash."

Carson shook his head in disbelief as he pulled twenty dollars from his pocket.

"I didn't even want to come here." He made it known. Carson headed to the bar, to two empty stools. He sat down, noticing his friend wasn't with him. He found Michael sitting at a small table, just off of a side dance stage.

"What are you doing?"

"You don't want to sit at the bar. The women expect tips as they make their way around, and I don't plan on dropping any ones like that."

Carson's mouth dropped open. He couldn't believe his ears. "You're a piece of work."

Michael smiled, taking it as a compliment. "That's why you hang with me."

Once Carson got settled, he observed his surrounds. The main stage was in the center of the bar. Girls were performing on the main stage and two side stages, about twenty-five feet on either side. The place was pretty packed, even for a Saturday. Carson was surprised how many women were in the club with their men. He wondered if Ebony would ever come to a place like this with him . . . although it wasn't really his scene.

A half-dressed, not very attractive server approached them to get their drink order.

Carson was reluctant. "I can only have one, because I exceeded my limit about two hours ago."

Michael laughed. "You're fine, man! What's the worst that can happen if you get drunk, you have a good time?" Michael continued to laugh as the server returned with cocktails.

The DJ's voice came over the loudspeaker. "Coming to the stage, put your hands together for Sugar!" An outpour of cheers and hollers came from the horny men in the audience. Even a few women stopped to see her walk out. Carson was in awe. A five-foot-five woman arrived, wearing five-inch clear platform shoes and a white nurse's outfit. Carson was already salivating. All the men watched her climb to the top of a pole, hang upside down by her thighs, then flipped off the pole into a split on the floor.

"Now *that* is a woman." Carson pulled out as many ones as he can find.

"It's her profession. You sound like you're about to propose."

Carson laughed. He knew if he were single, he might have to try to take her to bed, at least. Carson's became serious. "Can I ask you a question?"

"What's up?"

"Do you believe in oral sex?" He nodded towards Sugar, who was laying on her back with her legs open, gyrating what lay between her legs.

"Yeah! Don't you?"

"No. I'm scared."

Michael burst out laughing. Carson shoved him.

"That's why I don't talk to you. I'm trying to be real and you're laughing at me."

Michael covered his mouth. "Sorry man, I just don't know how you please your wife if you don't eat a little something extra. Trust me, if it doesn't feel good to her, she'll tell you what to do."

Carson looked back at his friend wondering if he was really giving good advice, or if he was blowing smoke again.

"It just seems so dirty."

Michael leaned back on his stool, laughing hysterically. "Oh shit. I'll be right back." Michael ran towards the bathroom.

"I hope he goes in his pants." Carson muttered.

One of the dancers walked up to Carson and shook her butt in his face. He slipped her a dollar to make her go away.

"It's okay if you smack it," she whispered in his ear.

Michael returned with Sugar right behind him. She grabbed Carson by the hand, and led him back to a private room. Carson looked back at his friend to save him, but the smile on Michael's face proved he'd be no help. Twenty minutes later, Carson returned with the dopey, after-sex grin on his face. Sugar leaned over and gave him a kiss on the cheek.

"I should cuss you out for that. But I'll thank you, instead."

Chapter Thirty-Four

"A fternoon, sis."

Ebony picked her head off the sofa to face India. Her head throbbed, and the sunlight was blinding, but she could see the digital clock that read 1PM.

"*Oh shit!* That's the right time? Why'd you let me sleep the day away?"

India laughed at her sister. "After last night, I thought you should sleep off all that booze."

Ebony laid her head back down, smiling as she thought back to the night at the club. She hadn't had that much fun in a long time. The last time she stayed out all night, she and Carson had just started dating. They'd caught the train to Harlem and went to a club. That was her introduction to Tequila, which bought her a full day of sickness . . . but she let herself go and danced the night away. She knew Carson was there to make sure nothing happened to her.

India looked at her quizzically. "So what exactly were we celebrating, last night?" Ebony slipped off the couch and ran to her purse.

"I forgot! I have something to play for you."

She put her CD in the stereo and pressed 'play'. India started bumping her head to the beat.

"I like this. Who is it?"

". . . Me."

India's jaw dropped. "*What?*"

Ebony couldn't contain her excitement. "That's why I came to the city! I met with a record producer and recorded my first single, yesterday. He gave me a contract, and I need to have a lawyer look at it, but he wanted me to sign to his label!" Ebony started jumping up and down.

"Is he for real?"

"*Please* don't go ruining my joy by being negative." Ebony sat back down.

"I'm not being negative. I'm a *realist* and I don't want you to get screwed." She saw the disappointment on her sister's face, and dialed her tone down a notch. "But if you feel this is real, then I'm happy for you."

Ebony smiled again.

"But you know *who* won't be happy . . ."

Ebony frowned, knowing her parents were going to give her a long lecture and do everything they could to persuade her not to sing.

"That's a lecture I'll have to put up with."

"So now what? Are you going to quit your job, or what?"

"Can I just enjoy my time in the big city? I don't know what I'm going to do next."

Ebony walked past her sister to the bathroom, to take a shower. India took out her espresso machine and started making one for her sister. She laid the cup for Ebony, for after shower. A few minutes later, Ebony sat on the kitchen stool and took a sip.

"This is delicious, thank you."

Ebony checked her phone and saw a message from her husband. She brought the phone close to her chest, thinking of how she missed Carson. But she felt she was on the verge of a new life, and wondered if he was meant to be a part of it.

"I feel like shopping."

"Well, get dressed, cause I know all the spots to hit."

They spent the day together, shopping, eating lunch, and just enjoying each other's company. Ebony and her sister had always lived very different lives. Melody had always been closer to her than her own sister. When they were younger, Ebony never had time for her sister because she was too busy with her own life. But as they'd gotten older, she regretted the distance between them. She felt India held that against her, creating that space between them. Their day together meant so much to Ebony to spend meaningful time with her sister, at last.

Chapter Thirty-Five

Jefferson slammed down his phone, failing to get a contract for his cyber security business. This was the third time that month that he'd been turned down, due to his lack of credentials.

"That damned Carson . . ." He pounded his desk, feeling that if he'd have never been kicked out of college, his business would be at the level he needed it to be.

Now he's messing with my money, he thought. *I need that woman to leave him . . . Maybe I should hurt him in his pockets as well. But how? All I know is that I need to take him down. Now!*

Jefferson picked up his phone and dialed his producer friend.

"How was this weekend? . . . Uh huh. Did she believe you? . . . Okay, well get that contract signed. Hopefully she won't be smart enough to have someone look at it too closely."

Jefferson hung up the phone and leaned back in his chair. He smiled, enjoying his years of hard work, plotting his revenge on Carson. Finally, it was coming together. It wouldn't be long before the Brody family fell apart, and knew the pain of failure that Jefferson had suffered for so many years.

Chapter Thirty-Six

Sunday evening was hit by a storm like no other. The summer heat brought strong winds, heavy rain, and a blackout that left half the state in darkness. Her train had reached the station just fine, but driving home from there was a problem.

The fat, heavy rain make it very hard for Ebony to see the road in front of her. The streets were dark, and she swerved all over the road, trying not to hit every branch in the road. All she wanted to do was get home to her husband and try to get her life back on track, even if the outcome was that a lifelong relationship came to an end.

In a flash, her thoughts were interrupted by a pair of oncoming lights. She started honking her horn as the lights come closer. The driver didn't react. The lights were headed straight for her. At the last second, Ebony jerked her car to the right. Her car swerved off the road, right into a tree. Her head slammed forward, hitting the steering wheel, then rebounded back against the headrest. She sat there, unconscious, with blood dripping down the side of her face.

Carson checked the time on his phone. It was close to 10PM. He worried because he knew his wife couldn't drive in bad weather. He called Ebony's phone, which just kept ringing through to voicemail. *Of course* her mailbox was full, because the *responsible* thing to do was listen to her messages and erase them. He called India next, to make sure Ebony didn't change her mind about coming home.

"Hey India. Do you have power?" He asked, concerned.

"Yes I do, thank goodness. How about you?"

Carson shook his head. "No. It's really coming down here, and I wanted to check on Ebony."

"She's not here . . . I put her on the train hours ago. The train was supposed to get there about 2 hours ago."

Carson's worries grew darker.

"Did you call . . . ?"

Carson hung up the phone, to call the train station. The station reported that all trains had come in on time, and no more would leave until the storm passed. Carson grabbed his jacket and umbrella, about to run out the door, until common sense hit him. What if Ebony went to Jefferson, instead of coming home to him? He sat down to think his options through. What if his wife was really in trouble? What if she had her legs in the air and was screaming out Jefferson's name?

He shook his head, trying to banish the thoughts. Carson tried Ebony's cell phone again.

"*Hello.*" A deep voice answered the phone. Carson stared at the phone, as if he might see the owner of the voice at the other end of the line. It didn't sound like Jefferson, but he couldn't be sure.

"Hello?"

Carson became angry. "Who is this? Where's my wife?"

"I'm sorry, but this woman's been in an accident. I stopped to help her when you called."

"Where are you?"

Carson could hear a siren blaring in the distance on the other end of the line. "We'll probably be at the Greensboro hospital by the time you get here."

". . . Okay. Okay. Thank you. Thank you very much."

Carson ran out the house. The hospital was twenty minutes from their house.

❧

Carson parked the car and ran into the hospital. He grabbed the first person he saw.

"I need to find my wife, Ebony Brody. She was in an accident."

"Follow me," said the young black doctor.

They went through a pair of double doors, down a hallway into a huge room with curtains everywhere.

"The fourth curtain." Carson slowly pulled back the curtain, hoping not to see anything horrible . . . and there she was. Ebony lay in bed with a bandage around her head and a few cuts on her face. Her eyes were closed, and all Carson could think was, *What if her eyes don't open?*

Looking at her, the memory of her walking down the aisle popped into his head. He remembered how beautiful and innocent she was, and all the love he had in his heart for her. At that moment, all the lies, cheating, and deceit didn't matter anymore. All that mattered was that she opened her eyes and looked into his. He wanted to tell her he was sorry for everything, and wanted to start fresh.

Carson sat in the lone chair by her bedside, and put his hand over hers. He laid his head down on top of their hands and cried, feeling her pain. The tears fell on her hand. Ebony groaned as the pain medication wore off. Carson lifted his head.

"Hi."

Ebony cocked her head to the side and gave Carson a half smile. "How are you feeling?"

127

"I'm okay, I think."

Carson squeezed his hand. "I'm *sorry*. This is all my fault and all the hurt we've brought each other . . ."

Ebony raised her finger and put it t her husband's lips to silence him. Deep down, she knew she was the only one that should apologize, because whether she was tempted or not, she should never have acted on her desires. If she still wanted to sleep with other men, then she shouldn't have made an oath to her husband.

Chapter Thirty-Seven

$\mathcal{E}$ bony had been discharged from the hospital. The torrential rains continued into the morning. Ebony managed to sleep, in her own bed, through the booming thunder. Her big brown eyes opened when her husband brought her a small tray of fruit, yogurt, and juice.

"What's this?"

"Breakfast. This is how I should've been waking you every day since we got married, and it's my fault. I turned you away, because I didn't spoil you like I should have. When I first saw you in the hospital bed, I swore if I ever got the chance to love you again, you'd never want for anything in the world . . . and I *meant* it. We deserve a fresh start."

Carson leaned over and kissed her deeply. The kiss made him want to climb on top of her and make love to her like never before, but he knew he needed to wait until she felt better. Still, he wanted to please her physically in *some* way. Carson moved the tray of food to the side of the bed, and kissed his wife on the lips once more. He slid his hand down her body and pulled off her panties.

His tongue ran down her body, slowly kissing every inch of her. Ebony shifted her weight, hoping what she wanted from her husband was really going to happen. He put his face beneath the covers and kissed her second set of lips. Her eyes rolled back in her head as she closed her eyes and enjoyed every minute.

A little while later, Carson peeked his wet lips up from out of the covers.

"I love you," Ebony managed, half out of breath. "I've been waiting for you to do that for *years.*"

He smiled, wiping his face. "So I did a good job?"

Ebony smiled and pulled his face close, to kiss him.

"You did great."

Although she felt a bit groggy from her medicine, Ebony pulled her husband on top of her, and made love to him like they were eighteen again—sneaking around in her parent's house.

Chapter Thirty-Eight

The headache ended a few days later, and Ebony was back to her old self again. Walking through the doors of her mom's office, she felt like a stranger; she hadn't been there in over a week.

"Nice to have you back!" Jessica said, standing to greet her.

"Thanks."

Ebony settled in behind her desk. There was a huge stack of folders waiting for her. The top one read 'Mrs. Carmine'. Ebony opened it, looking Mrs. Carmine's picture. She started to get misty-eyed as she thought of a way to honor Mrs. Carmine and tell her story, so other women could avoid her fate.

"Knock, knock."

Ebony looked up and saw Samantha in her door way.

"Now there's a face I haven't seen in a while." Ebony rushed over and gave her a hug.

"How have you been?" Samantha asked.

"I'm good. I just came to drop this off for you and your mother." Samantha handed over a fancy envelope.

"What is this?" Ebony opens it and saw a wedding invitation. Samantha can't hold her excitement in.

"He's a partner at another law firm. *So* fine, and he is *killing* it in bed. This man is everything. I can't wait for you to meet him."

Ebony opened her arms and embraced Samantha. "I wish you the best. And you can bet we'll be there."

Samantha pointed to the desk. "Tell the doctor thanks, and she can bury my file. I'm cured." She winked at Ebony and walked out.

Ebony struggled over her future, for a while now. She didn't want to work for her mother forever, and if she signed the contract with Leo, she hopefully wouldn't have to work two jobs anymore. There only seemed like one logical thing to do.

Chapter Thirty-Nine

s a last attempt to salvage their marriage, Ebony asked her mom's office mate, Dr. Richards, to counsel the two of them. Carson met his wife at 6PM. He was reluctant to see a therapist because he was such a private person, but since it meant so much to his wife, he agreed.

"Hi, Dr. Richards." Ebony gave her a hug, and Carson shook her hand.

"Have a seat." They followed her hand over to the tan leather couch.

Dr. Richards took her own seat. "So why are we here?"

Ebony looked at Carson to see if he wanted to start, but he returned the look so she starts the session.

"We haven't been married a year yet, and there are already major infidelity issues."

Carson chimed in. "That's because she is attracted to aggressive men, and doesn't know how to say no."

Ebony's jaw dropped open as she listened.

"And what about you and Leslie?" Ebony spat back. "Do you want her?"

Dr. Richards put her hands up. "Okay, we don't want this to become a screaming match. Carson, why don't you start. Tell your wife what you're feeling." Ebony rolled her eyes and leaned back on the couch, annoyed.

"I slept with Leslie back in college, but that was it. I kept that secret, because I know Ebony hates her and I didn't want to hurt my wife. But I love her. I always have, *she's* the one not happy with our life."

Ebony felt bad, because her betrayal was so much worse than his. Carson was too loyal to do anything crazy.

Dr. Richards nodded. "Ebony?"

"Okay, I *am* attracted to Jefferson. It's more than that though. He brought out the music in me, which I'll always be thankful for. Carson is *safe*. He always had been, and I love his stability, but every once in a while, I need to live a little. And to be completely honest . . . I've *always* been promiscuous. I thought getting married would help me with that. Carson had known that side of me and had accepted me for *me* . . . I just don't think I'm being fair to him."

Carson sat there, motionless. Ebony feared she'd said too much, that she broke her husband's heart; but it did feel good to finally say everything that had been on her chest since their wedding.

Dr. Richards turned to Ebony's husband. "Carson, are you okay?"

He slowly raised his head. Tears were in his eyes. "So why are you with me, Ebony?"

She came off the couch and knelt before her husband. She grabbed his hand and looked in his eyes.

"I love you. I have since you pushed me down and scraped my knee when we were *six*. I made a horrible mistake, and I'm truly sorry for that. I just want some *excitement* in our life. Not this kind, but we're young! We don't have kids yet, so we should be *enjoying* life while we still can."

Dr. Richards chimed in. "So, *both* of you have been unfaithful and lied in your marriage. Now we need to get past this, and focus on just the two of you."

Ebony climbed up off the floor and sat back down next to her husband.

"I don't know if I can change and be the man that *excites* her. I am not that guy."

"I'm not *asking* you to change yourself. I know that we'll always be financially secure, and our house will always be clean, and I'll always be taken care of because you're stable. All I'm asking, is that we go out sometimes, be more spontaneous, and maybe spice up our sex life a little."

The doctor nodded in agreement. "Now that the truth is out in the open, the *important* thing is not to bring any of it back up if you want your marriage to survive. You can't throw any of this back in each other's face, after today. If you want to walk out of this office with a clean slate, then you accept each others faults with forgiveness, and move on."

Ebony faced her husband, and he did the same. She reached her hands out for his. He sat very still, but his eyes were racing back and forth. Carson struggled, wondering if he could really leave all her betrayals behind . . . or would he see Jefferson's face every time they made love? He wondered if he was satisfying his wife they same way Jefferson did. Carson stood, leaving Ebony's empty hands on the couch. Tears spilled down her cheeks as she feared her husband would truly leave her.

"Carson!" She cried out.

He shook his head. "I need some *time*. You can't expect me to make a decision about my whole life in a single hour. Not with all this to work through."

He walked out of Dr. Richard's office. Diane crossed to the couch with Ebony, and held her as she wept.

Ebony finally returned home after talking to the doctor for a while longer. Dr. Richards told her she needed to break all ties with Jefferson and focus one hundred percent on her husband if she wanted it to work. Ebony sat at home alone for hours, watching TV in the living room. She feared that Carson had had enough of her wild ways and would tell her that it was over when he came home. She heard the front door open around midnight. Ebony stood up, facing the door, but the flickering light from the TV blinded her view. She saw Carson walking to her. The smell of alcohol hit her nose as soon as he was in arm's length.

"Are you okay?" she asked.

Carson never uttered a sound. He grabbed his wife and pulled her nightgown off her. He scooped her off her feet and stretched her out on the carpet.

"You're so beautiful." He said, looking at her nakedness.

Carson took an ice cube out of the glass of water, sitting on the coffee table. He ran the ice cube from the top of her neck down to her belly button, then licked the water off of her. Ebony moaned with pleasure. She smiled because her husband had come back to her. Carson made love to his wife on the middle of the floor. Ebony wrapped her legs around her husband, holding him tightly inside of her.

"I'm never going to let you go again," she promised.

Chapter Forty

*E*bony caught the early train into the city. She asked a lawyer client of her mother's to look over the singing contract. Wearing a blue power suit, Ebony strolled down Broadway, whistling and smiling. In her briefcase was the beginning of her new life. She and Carson were finally on the same page, and their love life was better than ever. Jefferson hadn't been a thought in her head for days, now, and it felt *good*. On the busy street, Ebony wasn't even paying attention to her surroundings when she bumped right into a big cushioned belly.

"Ebony?"

She looked up and saw Joe, the sound technician that recorded her first single.

"Where are you rushing to?"

She leaned in and hugged him, happy to see a familiar face in the busy city.

"Actually, I'm on my way to see Leo with my contract!"

Joe made an unpleasant face. Ebony looked at him, puzzled.

". . . What's wrong?"

"Have you signed it yet?"

Ebony wasn't sure how to answer the question. "Is there something you need to say to me?"

Joe looked around like he was being followed. Ebony followed his gaze to see what he was looking at.

"Did you have a lawyer look at it?"

"She's a family attorney, but yeah. Joe, please just spit it out."

Joe grabbed her arm and ducks into the nearest coffee shop. The two sat down at a small table. Joe put his hand on top of hers.

"I believe you've got real talent, and I know Leo does too, but there's someone who paid Leo a lot of money to make you fail."

Ebony shook her head, still not quite understanding what was going on.

"I just feel this isn't the right direction for you."

Her emotions began to run hot. "But . . . I don't know anybody else in the industry. Who would—?"

Joe reached in his pocket and slid her a business card across the table.

"Tell him I sent you."

Ebony got up and hugged Joe, thanking him. She still doesn't understand what was going on, but there was something brutally honest in Joe's eyes.

"So what do I say if Leo calls me?" she asked.

"Tell him you found a loophole in the contract. That'll burn him up."

Ebony nodded to thank him and walked out. There must have been *something* in the contract that the lawyer didn't see, but why would Leo do this to her, and who would want to hurt her like this? Ebony called the number on the card Joe gave her. He was a club owner, and he asked Ebony to stop by. Since she was only a few blocks away, she went right over to his club.

Ebony walked up to a red awning that read *Shannon's*. She looked down at the card, it read the same. She went inside, and to her surprise, Mr. Daniels was sitting right at the bar waiting for her.

"Are you the lovely lady Joe said I just have to meet?"

Ebony extended her hand. "I certainly hope so."

They shook hands. Ebony dug into her briefcase to pull out her single CD. Mr. Daniels picked it up and tossed it aside.

"I don't want to hear that, I want to hear *you*."

He snapped his fingers, and the stage lights came on. There was a sexy woman sitting behind the black grand piano on stage, and a single microphone. Ebony cleared her throat, put her bag and purse down, and proceeded to the stage. Ebony whispered to the piano player, and she started playing *I'm Going Down*. She sang like it was her last song ever. All the love she had for her husband, all the hate she had for Jefferson, all the excitement of her possible career and all the respect she had for the many people who were helping her out came out in her song.

After her last note and last drop of sweat left her body, Mr. Daniels stood and started clapping his hands. The lady at the piano nodded and smiled in approval. "I'll play with her any day," she said as she got up from the piano, and walked off behind some curtains.

"So can I sign you for three nights a week?"

He produced a contract and put it on the bar. Ebony rolled her eyes at the sight of another contract.

Mr. Daniels reassured her, "You can't trust everyone in this business, and trust me, I learned that the hard way. A contract protects both of us."

She looked in his eyes and something told her to trust him. She pulled the contract to her and looked it over. Mr. Daniels pulled out a pen and laid it down. She signed the contract for a year.

"And you can call me Marc."

She shook his hand and grabbed her stuff.

"Give your measurements to Nina in the back, and she'll find some costumes you can choose from. [Editor note: this seems incomplete. Who is Daniels talking about?] and he is expecting your call. I already gave him a copy of your single from Joe."

Marc handed her a business card. It seemed she was starting a collection.

"See you Saturday."

~~~

Jefferson watched as Ebony left the club and headed back to Grand Central Station. He took his cell phone and calls Leo, curious about what Joe had said to her.

"Have you heard from Ebony?"

"She texted me, saying she had to decline my offer, and thanked me for the opportunity."

Jefferson grew angry. "And where's Joe?"

"Strange thing. He quit this morning."

"I'll bet he did."

Jefferson hit the 'End' button, realizing Joe turned Ebony on to the truth. He felt that it was a perfect plan for her to quit her job thinking she had some big record deal, only to find out that the label would drop her if she didn't sell any records. And if Leo wasn't promoting her album, then she'd have lost out entirely. Jefferson knew he was going to the extreme just to take down Carson, but if Ebony had just left her husband to be with him, none of it would be happening.

Chapter Forty-One

Saturday evening, Ebony dragged her husband to the city which was something he hated to do. But since their counseling session, he'd been doing everything he could to make their marriage work. Carson liked his regular, peaceful life, so to be out in New York on a Saturday night was driving him crazy.

"Ebony, you know I can't stand these crowds."

Ebony had her husband's hand and dragged him through the streets.

"Shut up and trust me!"

Carson's eyes grew big. His wife had never told him to shut up with any seriousness. She finally let his hand go when they arrived at *Shannon's*. To her surprise, Joe was at the door, this time as the bouncer. He had a black eye and a scratch on his face.

"What happened, Joe?"

"I guess we were being watched the other day, but it's okay. I'm a big buy and I can handle myself."

Ebony felt terrible, because she thought it was her fault that Joe got beaten up.

"I'm sorry."

"I'm not," he replied. "Go make all this *worth* something."

Ebony leaned over and kissed Joe on the cheek, then realized Carson was standing there, feeling a bit in the dark.

"This is my husband, Carson."

The two men shook hands. Carson looked worried, not knowing what was next.

The club was packed, and Ebony felt nervous and excited at the same time. Marc waved her over to a small table for two. She introduced Carson, who was getting annoyed at meeting all these different men that knew his wife.

Marc disappeared after showing them to their table. "Ebony, please tell me what is going on."

"Just sit back and order a drink. It's on me."

Ebony kissed Carson on the forehead, and ran backstage to get ready. Shifting back and forth in his seat, Carson was uncomfortable, looking around at the happy couples around him. Twenty minutes later, a jazz group came on and did a fifteen-minute set. He sipped his glass of red wine, calming his nerves. He looked around for his wife, who had been gone a long time. His waitress ran right over.

"Do you need something, sir?"

"Yeah. I'm trying to find my wife so we can order some food!"

"Oh, I'm sorry. I can bring you something to munch on while you wait for her."

Carson smiled and nodded appreciating her kindness. He stood up to look for his wife when the waitress came back quickly with an order of chicken quesadillas. Carson thanked her, wondering how she knew they were his favorite appetizers.

He turned back to the stage as he heard his wife's name announced over the loudspeaker. He saw his wife walk out onto the stage, wearing a beautiful, sexy, red sequined dress, holding a microphone. His mouth dropped open.

Ebony nodded to the band and started to sing. He dropped his food onto his plate and leaned back in his chair. His eyes watered up, thinking back to the first time he'd heard her sing, back in high school at a talent show. Carson watched her work the stage and captivate her audience. Ebony was *glowing*. He hadn't seen his wife like this in years.

Marc put his hand on Carson's shoulder. "So what do you think?"

"I love that woman," was all he could manage.

"I'm starting to, too." Carson gave him a look. "Not in that way."

He relaxed and smiled at Marc. He patted his back and walks off.

Ebony sang three more songs before walking offstage. Fifteen minutes later, she came out into the restaurant. Carson saw her walking through the audience greeting her fans. She made her way to him, and he stood to greet her.

"You . . ." He shook his finger at her, then grabbed her in a huge bear hug. "You were *amazing*. How could you keep this from me?"

Ebony shrugged. "I'm sorry, it just happened so quickly, and I didn't want to jinx anything . . . Then I just wanted it to be a surprise."

He let go of his wife and pulled her chair out for her. The waitress brought Ebony a glass of water. Carson watched her as she drank, taking in his wife's every movement. The pleasure in her eyes told him how happy she truly was. The slowing beats of her heart showed how relaxed she was, and her smile showed that she was proud of herself, and rightly so. There had only been a few memorable moments in her life that made her truly proud.

Chapter Forty-Two

"Bitch, where you been at?"

Ebony looks at the phone in disbelief. "Well hello to you too, Melody."

"I haven't seen you in forever."

"Well, come by the office today. I could use your help."

It was moving day. Ebony had her hands full with packing boxes, as she tried to squeeze through the office door.

"Hello, beautiful."

Ebony screamed, dropping the boxes to the floor.

"What are you doing here, Jefferson?"

"I could ask you the same thing."

She scrambled around, trying to recover her boxes. Jefferson hadn't entered her mind in over a week, until she saw him standing in the doorway, reminding her how fine he looked. Still. She was in no mood.

"Like I said. What are you doing here?"

Jefferson stepped closer with aggressive strength. "You don't return my texts or call me anymore . . . What's up, girl? I know you need some more dick. You can't go too long without it."

Ebony shook her head. "I'm good, actually. And we're done. This was a mistake from the beginning, and I'm ending it. Now."

"How would your *husband* feel if he knew about our affair?" Jefferson reached out and touched her cleavage that was showing. Ebony swatted his hand away.

"Why don't you tell him and *find out*."

Jefferson looks into her eyes trying to see why she was calling his bluff. Ebony walked to the door, hoping Jefferson would follow. He walks to the door, only to slam it shut.

Jefferson grabbed her arm and turned her to face him. He pushed her up against the door and started kissing her neck. She pulled away.

"But I love you, girl! Does that mean nothing to you?"

Usually, the sound of a man uttering those words would make her panties slip off, but somehow hearing it from Jefferson's lips didn't mean anything real. Not anymore.

Her mother walked out of her office hearing the commotion.

"I believe she asked you to *leave*."

Ebony looked at her mom, amazed. Never being one to stand up for Ebony, her daughter was very proud of her for finally coming to her defense.

Melody pushed open the door, almost knocking Ebony and Jefferson aside. She looked in, seeing the two of them standing very close to each other.

"Am I interrupting something?"

"No," said Dr. Lovely, "he was just leaving."

Jefferson looked all three women up and down before leaving. Ebony slammed the door behind him. Her mother gave a slight nod and a smile at her daughter before returning into her office. Melody didn't hesitate.

"Spill it, bitch."

"Stop saying the b-word while I'm at work."

"Sorry . . . hussy." Melody gave her best friend a hug. "It feels like I haven't seen you in forever."

"I know! So much has happened."

Melody looked around the office. "Yes. What are you doing with all these boxes?"

"I'm packing. So grab a box."

Ebony picked a box up off the floor and handed it to Melody. She started putting photos in the box. Ebony started talking, from the beginning with her singing career and everything. She told her about the counseling session, and how she and Carson were stronger for it, and she was quitting her day job and moving on with her professional life.

Melody was stunned. "That's just amazing. I've got to come to Shannon's and check you out! I haven't heard you sing in years."

Ebony blushed. "I know, it's been great."

"I have some news, too . . ." Melody raised her left hand, exposing a huge two-carat diamond ring. Ebony had been so wrapped up in her own life, she hadn't even noticed.

"Is that what I think it is??" Ebony grabbed Melody's finger. "It's the same guy, right?"

"Yes!"

"Well, we need to celebrate! I can't believe *you* of all people are getting married."

"I know! I figured it had to happen sooner or later, right?"

Ebony couldn't stop grinning. "How exciting!"

Forty-five minutes later, her desk was all packed up. Ebony looked around the office, feeling she was leaving her mother high and dry . . . but it was time to start living her life. Melody left with the final box and loaded it in her car. Ebony stood in the doorway, reminiscing on the years she'd been there, and all the amazing women she'd met because of the job. One lonely tear fell from her right eye as she gave Jessica a hug, and closed the door behind her.

Chapter Forty-Three

Jefferson was in a panic as Leslie jumped out of her car running to her brother's side. "What is so *urgent* that you called me away from work?"

The man was livid. "Why haven't you landed Carson yet? I need your *help*."

Leslie slowed down. "You didn't really call me for this, did you? I don't want to be a part of your jealousy."

Her brother squints his eyes at her.

"Jealous?! I'm not jealous."

"Then let it go," Leslie pleaded. "College was over ten years ago."

"*You* graduated college. He took that from me, along with Angie. I just want him to lose everything important to him, the way I did."

Leslie looked at her brother, shaking her head. She knew he was missing a little something upstairs, and really wished he'd have continued with his therapy, years ago.

"Please. Just . . . put the heat on Carson one last time, and get him to sleep with you."

Leslie had always wanted Carson to be hers and that was no secret. But she didn't want to ruin a marriage. If the marriage was over already . . . that'd be a different story.

She hung her head. "He loves his wife."

"I've been with her. The way her body responds to me? I can't *believe* they're that happy."

She looked at her brother, seeing the desperation in his eyes. As kids, she'd always hated the way he got everything, and she always got the short end of the stick. Once again, she felt herself giving into her brother. It burned her up inside, yet she always seemed to give in.

She gave in. "I'll try, Jefferson. But I can't make you any promises. This is your mess . . . not mine."

Chapter Forty-Four

The excitement of recording an album was the only thing on Ebony's mind. Carson was in full support of his wife, putting his frugality aside. They dipped into their savings to get an entertainment lawyer to accompany her to her meeting with Mr. Daniels' friend. The meeting was everything Ebony thought it could be, and more. The contract was legitimate this time, and Ebony signed a three-album deal. Her life was going better than she'd ever expected. The minute she left the meeting, she called her husband who promised that they were going to celebrate.

"I'll make a reservation for tonight. I am so proud of you, baby!" Carson hung up the phone. Ebony texted Melody to make sure she'd be there. While she was still in the city, Ebony stopped in to a little boutique in Manhattan, to pick up a new dress. For the life of her, she couldn't stop smiling. Several hours later, Carson was home, ready to take her out on the town.

"So who's coming tonight?" She asked, putting the finishing touches on her makeup.

Carson peeked his head out of the bathroom with a toothbrush jutting out of his mouth. "Don't get mad . . . but I invited your parents and your sister."

"My parents! I haven't told them yet!"

"What did you tell your mom when you quit? She must know *something's* going on."

"I told her I was going back to school."

"You know how I feel about lying. So this is the perfect time to come clean."

She squinted her eyes, feeling agitated. He blew her a kiss and ducked back into the bathroom to finish brushing his teeth.

❧

"Brody reservation," Carson told the hostess as they arrived at 7:30PM.

The hostess led them to a table, where India and her parents were already waiting. Ebony gave her dad a hug; she hasn't seen him since the wedding.

"So what are we celebrating?"

"In due time." Carson smiled at his in laws as he pulled his wife's chair out for her. Melody and her new fiancé arrived a few minutes later. Carson ordered champagne for the whole table. The waiter poured everyone a glass.

"Well, I guess you're not announcing that we're going to be grandparents?" Her mom said, as she saw her daughter with bubbly in her hand.

Ebony laughed as she stands up. "I guess there's no time like the present."

Carson winked at his wife to show his support.

"Well," she took in a long breath, "I *signed a record deal* today."

India jumped up and started cheering in support of her sister, until her parents stared her down.

"What about finishing school?" her father asked.

"I might have told mom a white lie."

Her father shook his head, disapproving. Ebony's lip trembled.

"Excuse me,", she said, almost in tears, as she fled to the bathroom to compose herself.

"I don't mean any disrespect," Carson began, "but your daughter is extremely talented. I saw her perform the other night, and I've never seen her so happy. I *really* hope you can be happy for her. And if her singing doesn't pan out—and I think that it will—she can still finish school."

Carson got up and walked outside to get some air.

Ebony stood before the bathroom mirror, looking at herself. "I *will not* let my parents ruin this moment for me," she told herself. The door to the stall behind her opened, and Leslie walked out. Ebony rolled her eyes. Leslie was the last person she wanted to see.

"Fancy meeting you here," Leslie said with a devilish smile. "I noticed you're here with you family and husband, how nice."

"What do you want, Leslie?" Ebony turned to face the woman she despised.

"I was just astonished to see you here with Carson since you left him."

"Who told you that?"

"Your husband. The day you went to stay with your sister. I saw Carson that weekend. He told me everything."

Ebony wasn't having it. "Sorry to disappoint you, but I *didn't* leave him. I just went away for the weekend. And as you can see, we're stronger than ever."

Ebony washed her hands and crossed to the door. Leslie says rubs her lips sick together and made a kissing motion with her lips.

"So why was he was with me?"

Ebony heard Leslie laughing as she shut the door behind her. At the table, she returned to a different vibe. Her parents were sitting there, hand in hand, wearing the same small smile. Her father stood up.

"Sweetheart, if this is what you want, then your mother and I support you."

Her father walked to her and gave her a hug. Her eyes filled with tears, but they didn't fall. She looked down at Carson who was smiling up at her. She didn't return the smile.

"What's wrong?" asked Carson, as she returned to her seat.

"Why don't you ask *Leslie*?" Ebony grabbed her purse. "I'm sorry. I can't do this." She ran out of the restaurant to grab a cab home. Leslie was hiding behind a tree by the front door. She thought she would feel good, but she was actually hurt by the fact she was helping to wound a good friend of hers.

Carson darted out into the street, after his wife. He reached her arm as she waved it in the air to hail a cab.

"What is going on?"

Ebony turned to face Carson, livid. "Like I said, go talk to *Leslie* since you were with her the other last weekend!"

A taxi pulled up. Carson released his wife. She got in the cab, and in moments, she was gone. Carson watched the taxi's tail lights fade off into the distance. He couldn't wrap his mind around what just happened. As he made his way back into the restaurant, he saw Leslie slip in her car and drive off.

"What could she have possibly said to her? . . . And why?"

He was naïve to the fact that Leslie would do *anything* to have him all to herself; he didn't know Leslie was Jefferson's sister. Carson only knew where he had to go . . . and what he had to do.

By the time he reached the table, everyone had gathered their things. The night was over before it really got started.

The cabbie drove around in circles with no destination in sight. Ebony wanted to run to Jefferson. Her husband's betrayal was eating her up inside. But after she rejected him at the office the other day, it just didn't seem right. Carson seemed very quick to forgive her, and it all made sense if he was out cheating on her, then he couldn't be mad at her for doing the same.

Ebony finally directed the cab driver to take her home so that she could grab her car and some clothes.

Chapter Forty-Five

*M*elody smiled as she opened the door. "Somehow, I knew you'd end up here."

Ebony gave her friend a pathetic smile and let herself in.

"So what happened? Carson came back into the restaurant like he'd lost his best friend."

Ebony flopped on the couch. "He did."

Melody poured two glasses of wine and joined her on the couch.

"Well, I must say it was the best celebration I've been to in a long time," she said with a skeptical smirk.

Ebony wasn't in the mood for her friend's sarcasm. She picked up her bag and walked out of her apartment. Melody ran to the door after her.

"I was just kidding! Ebony, wait!" But she was gone. Ebony followed her first instinct and went to a motel where she could have some peace and quiet.

She settled into the Comfort Inn's small, dusty room. At that point, she could sleep in a barn, for all she cared. It wouldn't matter, as long as she didn't have to see or hear from anyone. She ran a hot bath and slid into the tub. Her cell phone sat on the toilet next to the bath. Every few minutes it lit up as Carson kept trying to call her, sending texts, pleading for her to answer the phone.

She closed her eyes trying to fully relax, thinking how her life had changed so quickly. Just a few days ago, she was so happy, and things were finally changing for the best . . . and now her life seemed to go crazy again. Deep inside, she knew that if Carson *did* sleep with Leslie again, she couldn't really hold it against him. Her own actions had been nothing short of unfaithful. The love she had for her husband ran deep and had been there a very long time, but maybe the two of them just weren't right for marriage.

Around midnight, she climbed out of the tub and laid down on the bed to watch some TV. Her phone was still buzzing, but this time the text came from Jefferson.

Still mad at me, beautiful? Ebony read the text and shook her head.

She texted back. *I was never mad. What I've been doing with you was wrong. I need to devote myself to my husband . . . but that probably backfired on me.*

Jefferson always seemed to interfere at the moment she was most vulnerable. He asked if he could keep her company, but she held her ground and said no. However, she *did* talk to Jefferson the rest of the night. She cheated one last time in a way she hasn't done before. Phone sex didn't seem as bad as physically cheating, but it still felt wrong.

Chapter Forty-Six

The house was empty when Carson drove by, so he kept going, straight to Leslie's house. His face was bright red as his anger surged in every part of his body. He was usually a peaceful man, but after pledging to make his marriage his top priority, he was in no mood to put up with Leslie jeopardizing that. He was ready to fight.

Part of him was praying she wasn't home so the fight didn't happen. But unfortunately, her car was there. He banged on her door, and she opened the door in a pink see-through teddy. Carson was taken aback at first, seeing Leslie's finely-toned body and perky nipples sticking out.

". . . We need to talk."

He pushed her front door open, and the wind lifted her teddy. Leslie looked confused, but she knows that moment was her last chance for Carson's love. She followed him in the house, shut the door and propped herself up on the side of the couch.

"What is it?" she asked with a smile.

He looked at her, trying to put his thoughts together. "Can you cover up, please?"

"Why, don't you see anything you like?" she rose, walking closer to him. He stepped back, feeling his manhood rise.

"Please?"

She walked off to grab a robe, shaking her head. After covering herself, she took her seat back on her couch.

"Just what did you say to Ebony tonight at the restaurant? And before you lie, I *saw* you there."

Leslie rolled her neck, deciding how she wanted to go about this.

"I've known you a long time, Carson. I don't know *why* you continue to run *after* this woman. You need a woman that'll be *honest* with you and can help bring you up, not cheat on you!"

Her words struck home. He knew part of her was right, but Ebony was a caring woman and he knew what they had was real.

"Answer the question, Leslie."

"Carson, I love you. I've loved you for years. And I would *never* betray you the way she has. Repeatedly."

He was getting angry, and she was avoiding the question. He grabbed her arms and shook her.

"Answer the damn question!!"

"I just said that I thought she'd left you because you told me she was with her sister."

He loosened his grip. She stood up and drops her robe.

"Why don't you want all this?" Leslie leaned in and kissed him. He returned the kiss . . . then pulls back.

Carson tried to be kind. "You know how much I think of you. You've been my friend for so long . . . and I respect and value that relationship."

Leslie stepped back and smiled as she listened. She dropped her teddy to the ground and stood there, nude. Standing there in her heels and nothing else, she drove him crazy. Carson's dick was rock hard, which Leslie noticed. She smiled even harder as she took a step to him and grabbed him. He grabbed her naked body, wanting to penetrate her, but his willpower and his conscience wouldn't allow him. He pulled her into a hug, so he couldn't see her nakedness. Leslie tried to unzip his pants as she lowered herself to her knees. Carson backed up and went to grab her robe.

"What does she have that I don't?"

He turned, looking at her flawless body. At that moment, his mind could think of only one thing.

"She had my heart."

Carson held out her robe for her to get dressed. Ashamed and embarrassed, Leslie took it and put it back on. Seeing the hurt in her eyes, there was nothing left for Carson to say. He gave her a soft kiss on the forehead. She sank onto her couch, defeated. She watched the man she loved walk to her door . . . where he stopped.

"What is this??" He pulled a framed picture of Leslie and Jefferson off the wall. "How the hell do you know him?" His rage came back as he threw the picture across the room, where it shattered against the wall.

". . . He's my brother."

Carson's feelings overcame him. He sank to the floor and started crying. Leslie joined him on the floor. She put her hands on top of his. Leslie started talking about when she and Jefferson were kids. She confirmed that Jefferson had planned his attack on Carson for years. Carson felt betrayed, but also relieved to have the truth come out.

"I'm sorry." Leslie looked into his eyes with true sincerity. "Go get your wife back."

She couldn't believe the words coming out of her mouth, but she'd survive. She knew that Carson couldn't live without Ebony.

Chapter Forty-Seven

he sky had a grayish blue tint; it was beautiful, but also scary at the same time. After leaving the motel, Ebony planned on going home and talking to Carson. But first she had to put everything to an end with Jefferson once and for all. Early that morning, she received a text from Carson, confirming that he hadn't slept with Leslie since college, and that he'd explain everything when she came home.

Ebony had a weird feeling running through her as she pulled up to Jefferson's townhouse. She wanted him to know that he no longer had anything over Carson, and that he needed to leave them alone for good.

Ebony reached up to knock on the door when she realized that it was already ajar.

"Hello?" She pushed the door open. The cool air from the outside circled around her and gave her a chill. Jefferson appeared out of nowhere, dressed in a black tank top and black sweat pants.

"So last night wasn't enough, you need the real thing?"

Ebony rolled her eyes.

"I need you to leave me and my husband alone. For keeps."

"Come in. Shut the door." She reluctantly followed his orders, but made sure the door stayed unlocked.

"Now, what makes you think you have that much power over me?" Jefferson asked.

"I know Carson cheated on me, but it's ancient history. So whatever it is you think you have over him, you don't. So leave us alone." Ebony felt she was in over her head. She'd never felt this much fear in his presence. She'd been nervous before, but it was more of an excited fear.

"You really think it's all about *him* cheating on *you*. I don't care about that. I'd say good job, because his tight ass had never done anything wrong in his *life*."

"Then what do you want with us??"

Jefferson had a rictus smile on his face. "Oh, I got what I wanted from you . . . and now I've hurt Carson hurt like he hurt me . . . but I haven't taken everything from him yet. Not completely. I still have to make him *suffer*, like he did me."

A confused look came over her face. She felt stupid because she'd helped Jefferson hurt her husband without even knowing about his long-term plans.

"Why do you want to be married to a bitch? The fact that you're here with me instead of with him . . . shows you something. You need a *real* man. That's why you keep coming back because your man can't do the things I can." Jefferson grabbed his package.

Ebony turned to leave knowing she shouldn't have come. Jefferson grabbed her hands, pinning them behind her back. He pushed her down on the steps to the left of the front door. Part of her wanted to feel Jefferson inside of her one last time, but the pain overwhelming her heart wouldn't allow it. He picked up her vulnerable body and dragged her up the steps to his bedroom. He tossed her across the bed like a rag doll.

Jefferson parted her legs, ripping off her red lace panties and forcing two fingers inside her to feel her moisture. Jefferson smiled, knowing that as much as she resisted, she wanted him just the same. Tears fell from her eyes as she screamed out for him to stop.

"Shut up! This is what you want from me."

Ebony smacked Jefferson across the face as he loosened his pants. He grabbed her arms and put them above her head. She knew he was much too strong for her to break free. He forced his dick inside her, moving faster and faster, enjoying every moment. She was flooded with painful feelings. Jefferson pulled out, flipped her body over and pushed her face into his pillow, grabbed her butt and fucked her from behind. Droplets of sweat fell from his face, onto her back. The sound of their bodies slapping together filled the room for the next several minutes.

Jefferson groaned and grunted as he pulled out and released his load all over her back. He got up and walked to the bathroom to clean himself off.

"Dirty bitch," he muttered. The once classy lady lay face down motionless on the bed. He returned a few minutes later to find the bed deserted.

"Ebony?" He said sweetly, as if they were playing hide and seek. "Come on out . . ."

Ebony was down in the kitchen, scrambling for a knife. In her search, she spotted a picture of him, Leslie, and Carson back in college. Something in her brain clicked. Jefferson coming back into their life was no accident. Since the night before her wedding, he'd had a plan . . . But what? And why her?

Jefferson heard a drawer shut below as he slipped on some pants, and slowly crept down to the kitchen. He saw her standing in the kitchen, trembling. He pulled a penny out of his pocket and threw it at her, just to tease her.

She screamed, frightened and in shock. Jefferson slowly showed himself.

"What is your connection?" She asked, holding up the picture.

"Remember that stripper you slept with before you got married? I paid him, bitch. That's when I realized just how easy you really were."

He pointed to the knife in her hand. "What are you doing with that?" She said nothing as Jefferson stepped closer. She reached out with the knife.

"Don't come any closer." Jefferson still approached, knowing she wouldn't do anything. His steps became slower and slower as he came in arm's reach of her. Jefferson grabbed at the knife, just as Ebony slashed down, cutting his wrist.

Jefferson hollered out and backhanded her across the face. The impact swung Ebony in a circle as she fell to the ground, hitting her head on a cabinet on the way down. He stared at the blood oozing from his arm. She lay their motionless with a red bloodstain on her cheek. She was out cold. Jefferson leaned down, with the knife pressing against her body.

"*Why* would you fight so hard for that sorry ass husband of yours? You've had a taste of a real man. I ate your pussy so good that you forgot all *about* him, and yet you *still* want him." Ebony could only hyperventilate as fear saturated every nerve in her body. "Well, I hope you said your last goodbyes. He took the love of *my* life, and now I'll take his."

Jefferson started to drag Ebony towards the door when he heard a knock. He froze, waiting for the person to leave.

"Open the door, Jefferson." He recognized Leslie's voice. He dragged Ebony back into the kitchen and hid her, so she wasn't in view of the front door. He grabbed a towel and wrapped it around his wrist to hide the blood.

"What do you want?" He rushed to the door, to get rid of her quickly. He opened the door, and Leslie immediately sensed something was wrong.

"What happened to you??"

"Nothing! This is a bad time. I've gotta go." Jefferson started to shut the door, when a foot wedged in. He followed the foot up, and saw Carson, standing with his sister. Without a second thought, Jefferson punched Carson back. He slammed the door shut and ran back to check on Ebony, who was still unconscious.

He scooped her limp body off the floor without a plan in mind. He just needed to get rid of her for good.

Thud! Carson kicked the door open. Jefferson looked up with Ebony in his arms to see Carson and his sister coming at him.

"Put her down!" shouted Leslie.

"You? *You* of all people are sticking up for her? I can see *him*, but not you." He shook Ebony in his hands.

"What do you want with her??" asked Carson, fearing for his wife.

"This ain't about her. It's about *you* and how you ruined my life in college."

Carson shook his head in confusion. "What I *did*? *You're* the one who held me sleeping with Leslie over my head. *That's* why I kept you so close since you showed back up. Why do you think I invited you to the wedding? It sure as hell wasn't because I *wanted* you there!"

Jefferson put Ebony on the floor.

"You got me kicked out of college and ruined *everything* between Angie and me. So now I'll take everything from *you*."

He pulled out a switchblade and flicked it open, and put it to Ebony's throat. "Kiss your wife good-bye." He pressed the knife hard against her flesh. Ebony woke up.

"Baby hold on!" Carson started towards his wife.

"Don't come any closer," warned Jefferson. Ebony screamed out and started trembling in terror.

Jefferson grabbed her hair, yanking her head back. "Shut up!" He licked her neck and ran his hand down her chest, making Carson furious. "I'll miss this sweet ass. I've gotta admit you picked a good one."

Carson had never been so angry in his life. Leslie put her arm out to stop him charging at Jefferson.

"Carson didn't get you kicked out off school. *I* did."

Jefferson lowered his hand and stared at his sister in disbelief.

"Carson, I'm so sorry," Leslie implored. "Jefferson fell in love with a girl named Angela. She worked for the Dean of the criminal justice department. She fixed some grades for him and he had told you in confidence because you were roommates. Later, the dean found out, and they were *both* expelled. Angela never forgave him or spoke to him again."

Carson stared daggers at Jefferson. "So that's what this is about, you getting back at me? I thought you were going to tell Ebony about me and Leslie."

"I didn't even know the two of you were together at the time, I just knew my sister was in love with you." Jefferson looked at his sister.

"How could you do that to me?!"

"Because our whole life, you've had everything! You were *always* the one to succeed. I chose to go to NYU to live my *own* life. Then you followed me there and I was fed up with you! I needed my own success!"

Jefferson looked at his sister, eyes filled with betrayal. They'd always been close growing up, and to hear that his sister sabotaged his whole college career, it *hurt*.

"You watched me suffer *for years* because I had no college degree and couldn't get into another school . . . and you said *nothing*."

"That's right, I *did*. And I let you get your revenge on Carson, hoping they'd break up and I could have him all to myself."

Carson took two steps away from Leslie, realizing they *both* might be crazy.

"Man, I'm sorry. You should have come to me. I would've never betrayed your trust." Jefferson looked down at Ebony, feeling bad for the first time about what he'd done to her.

Leslie pulled a small silver-plated gun out of the back of her pants. "This can still end good."

"It's over, Leslie." She pointed the gun straight at Ebony. She tilted her head towards Carson, not taking her eyes off Ebony. "I'm

163

doing this for us!" She pulled the trigger at the same moment that Carson grabbed her arm, knocking her down.

Ebony screamed out and grabbed her shoulder. Jefferson ran to his sister, snatched the gun out of her hand. "I hate to do this to you sis, but don't move. Carson, call an ambulance for your wife."

Ten minutes later, Jefferson's house was filled with cops and paramedics. Ebony's shoulder had been wrapped up by the time she was loaded into an ambulance. The young female officer, first on the scene, put Leslie in handcuffs and escorted her to the back of her cop car. She handed Jefferson her card and winked at him on her way out of his house. Jefferson smiled back, and he checked out her ass in her fitted blue uniform pants.

He turned to Carson, filled with regret. "What can I say?"

Carson extended his hand, "Thank you for saving my wife." Jefferson returned his hand shake. "Just get your sister the help she needs."

Outside, the police office rapped the back of ambulance. The sirens started roaring and Carson made his way to his car to go meet his wife at the hospital. He pulled off, looking Leslie in the eye. He shook his head, no longer knowing the woman in handcuffs. He thought about all the turmoil in the mockery he'd called his life for the last several months. He drove off to reclaim his life, and his marriage. "I think it's time we took that honeymoon."